WALLS OF

BLUE COQUINA

HARCOURT BRACE JOVANOVICH, PUBLISHERS

SAN DIEGO   NEW YORK   LONDON

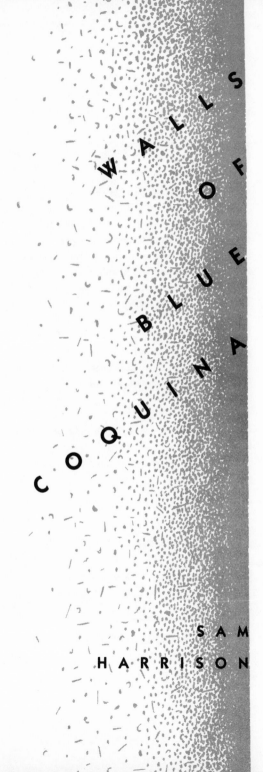

WALLS OF BLUE COQUINA

SAM
HARRISON

HBJ

Copyright © 1990 by Sam Harrison

All rights reserved. No part of this publication
may be reproduced or transmitted in any form or
by any means, electronic or mechanical, including
photocopy, recording, or any information storage
and retrieval system, without permission in
writing from the publisher.

Requests for permission to make copies of any
part of the work should be mailed to:
Copyrights and Permissions Department,
Harcourt Brace Jovanovich, Publishers,
Orlando, Florida 32887.

Library of Congress Cataloging-in-Publication Data
Harrison, Sam.
    Walls of blue coquina: a novel/Sam Harrison.
      p. cm.
    ISBN 0-15-194195-5
    I. Title.
  PS3558.A6719W35   1990
  813'.54—dc20   89-29206

Printed in the United States of America

First edition

A B C D E

Special thanks to my parents for all the books and music, to the Thursday Night Gang for their encouragement and criticism, and to the everlasting Gulf of Mexico.

For Barbara and Jesse,
who sacrificed

Co·qui·na 1: a small marine clam (genus *Donax*)
used for broth or chowder **2:** a soft whitish
limestone formed of broken shells and corals
cemented together and used for building
—Webster

The horizon is tormented by a wire fence.
The world is like something useless, thrown away.
It is still day in the sky, but night is lurking
   in the gullies.
All that is left of the light is in the blue-washed walls
   and in that flock of girls.
—Jorge Luis Borges
"Sunset over Villa Ortuzar"

WALLS OF

BLUE COQUINA

When Junior interrupted him, Bobby Sauls had finally seen how the world would be beautifully changed. It would begin there at the cluster of fourteen cottages by the Gulf of Mexico, according to the nebulous, eight-month-old prediction of Psychic Ike. Unlike Bobby's previous nine or ten visions, born of an unusually cold coastal winter and rainy spring and subject therefore to romantic moods, this one grew out of a seemingly endless stretch of clear, lifeless June days with the Gulf pulled flat and shiny like a green taffeta ribbon and the sky a constant blue. Though the withering heat had eliminated all but the most essential movement, Bobby Sauls was stirred to action by his enlightenment. He pushed himself out of his worn rattan chair and stood scanning the thin, purple horizon. The pain in his knees came again as his legs filled with blood. It was then that Junior bounded around the corner of the cottage in his gangly enthusiasm, leaped up the steps, and careened onto Bobby's porch.

"Granddad," Junior shouted, "Ronnie says he's gonna drown the baby if it ain't got the extra finger. He says as soon as it's born, if it ain't got an extra little finger on its right hand, that proves it ain't his and he'll drown it right out front here." He swayed on the balls of his feet like he was nailed to the porch floor, buffeted by a wind Bobby didn't feel. He looked expectantly at Bobby, with his eyebrows raised and his mouth open.

"So what do you want me to do about it?" Bobby snapped. "I can't worry about that now. I've got to see Ike. I know what it's going to be." He wanted to get to Ike before the image slipped away like the others and became a part of the long, curving line of the Gulf. Ike had to know about this one—see it in all its clarity and feel the excitement Bobby had felt when it appeared. But Junior's news was disturbing. The thing with Ronnie and Linda's expected baby was going too far.

"I can't do anything about that now," Bobby said. "Talk to me later. Where's Ronnie now?"

"It's Sunday afternoon," Junior said, hurt by the old man's stupidity. "He's sleeping, but he told me at lunch what he was going to do."

"I'll talk to him later," Bobby said, as he went out the screen door and down the steps into the hard sunlight. "I got to go now. He won't drown anything while he's asleep." He started walking toward Ike's cottage, leaving Junior standing behind in the heat.

"He means it," Junior called after him.

"Damn," Bobby said, and fixed his eyes on Ike's shimmering cottage. With the part of him that was still attached to family, he suddenly felt a pang of sympathy for his granddaughter, Linda, pregnant in this heat. And he almost let his thoughts fall into the whole humid entertainment of Ronnie's accusations, but then he remembered the flying fish, and the memory propelled him to Ike's screened porch.

In back of Bobby's cottage, away from the Gulf, the other cottages were situated among the few tall slash pines, in two rows of six each, forming a vee. Bobby's was at the point of the vee and closest to the thin strip of white beach. Yet another cottage sat at the far end across the brown grass and the heat. There, Bobby's wife, Mother Sauls, ran a little store for their guests and for the locals along that stretch of coast. The cottages were all of the same boxlike construction with a screen porch on the back, white painted tongue-and-groove siding, and blue shingled roofs. All but Bobby's were one bedroom. Linda and her husband, Ronnie, lived in one, Junior lived with Bobby and Mother Sauls, and Psychic Ike had a cottage to himself up by the road. No one else was there. It had been too hot, and people had stayed away.

Bobby could see Ike's huge form at a table in his darkened kitchen. His bulk nearly filled the soft rectangle of light showing from front to back through the cottage. Bobby could see the light in Ike's wild hair and beard as he bent over, reading or studying something. Bobby climbed the wooden steps, passing under a hand-painted sign that said Psychic Readings, opened the screen door, and went onto the porch.

"Ike," Bobby said. "I know what it's going to be. It finally came to me while I was on the porch looking at the water."

Ike loomed up from the kitchen table and met Bobby in the doorway. "That's all you ever do, man," Ike said.

"What makes this time any different? You're always bringing crazy ideas over here."

Bobby attributed the worn sound of Ike's voice to the heat and pushed his way past the big man into the tiny kitchen. "Because I wasn't trying this time," Bobby said. "I wasn't trying at all, and it came to me. In fact, I may have been asleep—did I tell you I sometimes can't tell the difference anymore? Anyway, it came to me very clearly, and now I know."

"Come in and sit down," Ike said. "Tell me what you know."

Bobby sat down at one of the chairs at the kitchen table. A deck of tarot cards was spread out in an arc on the tabletop. Ike stood over Bobby for a moment scratching his beard and then, like a trained bear climbing onto a bicycle, he straddled a chair across from Bobby. "So?" Ike said.

Bobby tried to organize the vision in his mind so he could talk about it, but all he could think of was the heat. He looked across the table at the imposing figure of Psychic Ike. "It's very hot," Bobby began.

"It's going to be hot forever, I think," Ike said with no malice. "What about the prediction?"

Eight months before, in the fall, Ike had come to this place on the Gulf with a dozen others on motorcycles. Bobby was the first to know about them, even while they were more than a mile from the cottages. It was the first really cool day of November, a morning of brilliant sunshine and clear blue sky, and Bobby had come out the front door of the store to stand and breathe in the smell of the fall woods across the road. He closed his eyes and took a long, deep breath, and then he heard a low rumble he thought at first was a large plane. He opened his eyes and searched the sky, and as the roar increased in volume, he could pick out the individual engines within it, and he knew it was coming on the road.

Bobby went down the porch steps and out into the road and looked toward the sound. He saw them round a curve onto the straight stretch that ran by the cottages, a column of low-slung motorcycles riding two abreast. Bobby stepped back off the road and watched them slow as they approached the cottages. One of the riders in the lead signaled with his hand, turned, and led the column into the yard. Bobby counted as they went past. There were nine cycles, four of which carried women riding in tandem, their arms locked around the middle of the man in front. One of the women waved at Bobby as they rumbled past, coming to a stop in the middle of the yard.

Mother Sauls came out of the store and stood wiping her hands on her apron. "What the hell is this?" she said.

"I don't know," Bobby said. "But I'm gonna find out."

"Be careful," said Mother Sauls.

The riders dismounted and stretched their legs as Bobby made his way across the yard. They were a tough-looking bunch, the men nearly all with full beards and shoulder-length hair, wearing dirty denims and riding leathers, and the women hard featured. Every machine was carrying bedrolls and saddlebags. The man who had signaled the turn came toward Bobby, removing his riding gloves. A long silver chain swung from his belt to his hip pocket.

Bobby stopped and waited for the man. "Howdy," he said. "What can we do for you?"

The man extended his right hand. He was about Ronnie's size and looked to be in his early forties, with a broad, flat nose and wide forehead. "Morning," he said, shaking Bobby's hand. "I'm Gypsy. If these places are for rent, we were wondering if you could put us up for a few days."

"I don't know," Bobby said. Mother Sauls had joined him and stood at his right elbow. "Depends. There's quite a few of you."

"Oh, we're used to doubling up," Gypsy said. "We don't require much. We can pay."

"You some kind of gang?" Mother Sauls interjected.

Gypsy looked at her and smiled. "No, ma'am," he said. "We're just a few working people on vacation, headed downstate." The others had formed a semicircle behind him and were watching Bobby and Mother Sauls.

Bobby looked at Mother Sauls and shrugged. "Well, we've got some empty places," he said. "It's kind of a slow time of year with the cooler weather setting in."

"We like a quiet place," said Mother Sauls. "And you pay for anything you break. I don't tolerate no hooliganism."

"Yes, ma'am," Gypsy said. "No problem. We won't break anything. We just want to enjoy the water for a few days."

"All right," Mother said. "Come on into the store and I'll sign you up. You can get some things to eat in there too. All the cottages have kitchens."

"Fine," Gypsy said. "Thank you, ma'am."

Bobby heard a screen door slap and he saw Linda making her way across the yard. One of the biggest bikers left the group and stood apart, looking down the line of cottages to the Gulf. He raised both hands over his head and let out a great, long laugh.

"What's he doing?" Bobby asked.

"That's Psychic Ike," Gypsy said. "He must be getting an impression, or something."

"An impression of what?" Bobby said. "Is he crazy?"

"No," Gypsy replied. "He's a fortune-teller."

"He's the damn biggest fortune-teller I've ever seen," Bobby said.

Psychic Ike put down his arms, turned around, and rejoined the group. He looked at Linda, who stood watching him with her hands on her hips, and then he spoke.

"I've just had a premonition," he said, in deep, rolling tones. "Just about the strongest one I've ever felt. Something very powerful and beautiful is going to happen here." He looked at each of the Sauls in turn. "Something that will change your lives forever."

"What are you talking about?" Linda asked. "What's going to happen here? When?"

"I can't see it clearly," Ike said. "But it's big. I've never felt anything so powerful as this." They looked at each other a long time, and then Linda lowered her gaze and looked at her feet. Bobby thought he had never seen a more imposing person than Psychic Ike. Something in him stirred as the resonant meaning of the big man's words took hold.

"Ike's generally right," Gypsy said. "He's the one told us there'd be a place to stay around here. Described it nearly perfectly too."

"Don't take no mind reader to know there'd be a place to stay somewhere on this coast," said Mother Sauls. "Come on, let's get you folks registered."

The riders stayed a week. Ike read palms and gave advice to the Sauls and their neighbors, and when the rest moved on, he decided to stay and set up shop in one of the cottages by the road so he could await the manifestation of his vision.

One afternoon, shortly after he moved in, Ike constructed a huge palm-shaped sign out of three sheets of four-by-eight plywood. He painted and lettered it and talked Mother Sauls into letting him erect it in front of his cottage to attract business. It worked, and now a steady, if thin, stream of neighbors came for advice and—Ike's specialty—to communicate with departed relatives. His prediction about the cottages generated considerable excitement in the family at first; but then, when nothing happened, when the rains came and went and the slow, ponderous heat set in, they easily and without ceremony accepted Ike as another eccentric addition to their little circle and forgot why he had decided to stay. Especially after the announcement that Linda was pregnant.

All but Bobby. Bobby sat on the screen porch by the Gulf, dreaming up scenarios to fulfill the prediction and presented each one to Ike over the kitchen table. Ike turned them all down. "Then, what will it be?" Bobby asked each time. "I can't see that," Ike would say. "I just know what it's not, and it's not what you've brought me so far."

Ike was just a little over six feet but carried more than three hundred pounds on his thick-boned frame. He had long, black hair, a full, tangled beard that showed more gray than black, and a wonderful array of tattoos on his arms and chest. Since the heat, he had taken to going without his emblematic black Harley Davidson tee shirt, showing the tattoo Bobby liked best, the one carrying all the way across: God Forgives. I Don't.

Bobby looked at Ike across the table again. "Do you

have any water or anything?" he said. "Some iced tea, maybe?"

"I've got beer," Ike said. "You want a beer? You shouldn't drink this goddamn tap water, man, it tastes like it came straight from the Gulf."

"Fine," Bobby said. "I'll have a beer. I'll tell you what I know."

Ike got up and went to the refrigerator, took out a beer for each of them, and handed one to Bobby.

"It will come from the water," Bobby said. "I know that. That's really all there is around here. I saw it today when I was nearly asleep, looking out over the water." He paused and took a sip of the beer, conjured the image again, and put the beer down firmly on the yellow Formica tabletop. "Flying fish," he said.

"What?"

"Flying fish," Bobby repeated. "It will start with one or two. We won't be able to see them at first because they're so small. And we won't think much of it at first either, except that you don't see them in close like this, but they're going to come sailing right in toward the cottages from the Gulf. They'll come flying and diving, and soon there will be hundreds and then thousands, and the air will be full of flying fish." He stopped and took another drink, then leaned across the table to Ike. "Do you know what I'm saying?" he asked conspiratorially.

"I've never seen one." Ike said. "I've heard of them, but I've never seen one."

"They're usually only way out," Bobby confided. "They come out of the water and fly along the bow of your boat. They have little wings, and they really fly. Sometimes they land in your boat, and that's the only way to catch them.

They're very good to eat, but there's no way to catch them unless they decide to land in your boat. And then it's not like really catching them, because they do it for you. Most of them are about the size of a good cigar."

"I've never been out in a boat," Ike said.

"Flying fish," Bobby said again. "Every flying fish in the Gulf is going to come in and land right here in this yard. It will take all day and all night, and in the morning you won't be able to walk around. They'll be piled up everywhere, all still flapping their wings and trying to fly off again. But they won't be able to because there will be so many. Thousands, maybe millions!"

He finished and leaned back in the chair, holding the beer but not drinking it, looking over the top of it at Psychic Ike. Ike stretched out both arms over his head and yawned. Bobby waited a minute more, but Ike said nothing.

"What do you think?" Bobby finally said.

"I'm thinking," Ike said slowly. "I told you I don't know how it's going to happen, just that it's going to happen here. It's not like reading a book, or watching TV, you know. It's more of a feeling. You say you've got the vision. Fine. Maybe you do, but I can't tell you if it's right or not. We'll just have to wait."

"It'll be soon," Bobby said. "I felt that."

"I think so too," Ike said. "But who knows." He tossed his empty beer can into the sink, where it bounced three or four times, but stayed, then got up and got another from the refrigerator. He held it out to Bobby, who shook his head no. "What makes you think what you've told me is so wonderful?" Ike said.

"My God," Bobby exclaimed. "It's pretty goddamn strange, don't you think?"

"Sure," Ike said, "but what makes it so wonderful?"

"Because we'll have seen it, that's all."

Ike got up again and walked around the kitchen. He stopped and looked out the back door at the Gulf. "Why flying fish?"

"That's what I saw," Bobby answered with some exasperation.

"I don't know, man," Ike said. "I'll have to think about it. Come back tomorrow and we'll talk about it some more. I'm taking the bike apart in the morning, so come after that." He looked at Bobby and smiled. He didn't look quite so ominous when he smiled. "Don't tell the others, though. This might not be it at all."

Bobby stood to leave. The beer had made him sleepy. "They don't care," he said. "They're all worried about the baby not having an extra little finger. Ronnie says he'll drown it if it doesn't." He felt the stiffness in his knees again. "But this is it. I know it is. Flying fish are going to come in and fill up the yard, and we'll get to see it, and it will be wonderful." He shook Ike's hand and went back out into the heat of the yard. No one else was in sight, but he heard music coming from the cottage where Linda and Ronnie lived. He did not recognize the music, and it grated against the flat calm of the Gulf and sky, and even against the brown grass of the yard. He would have to watch the Gulf even more, to be the first one to see them coming.

Bobby wiped the sweat from his brow with the extra little finger of his right hand and remembered Junior's warning. The picture of the flying fish looping into the yard faded, and it made him angry, so he tried to push away the thought about Ronnie and the baby. But it wouldn't go away. Not all the way. It got mixed up with the image of the flying fish, and he imagined Ronnie holding the baby under water while the fish flew over his head into the yard.

Someday he would talk to Ronnie about the baby, but not today. There was plenty of time. Bobby Sauls came to a stop under one of the pines that surrounded the cottages. He stuck both hands deep in his pockets, put everything back together in his mind the way he wanted it, and then shuffled over the dry grass to the cool haven of his own porch to await the flying fish.

"I'm going to write down everything that's ever happened to me," said Mother Sauls, who had joined Bobby on the porch. "I started this morning before breakfast with the very first thing I remember — my mother bathing me in a washtub in the yard."

It was the smoky purple evening of the day, and they sat watching the sun go down in the Gulf. When his wife spoke, Bobby was thinking how he hadn't seen himself in a mirror in years. He shaved by touch in the shower and always brushed his teeth looking out the window at the Gulf. He was seventy-two, but he still thought of himself as forty. He was trying to imagine what he really looked like.

What the others saw was a lean, hard, and brown old man of five feet nine inches, with close-cropped gray hair and deep blue eyes accentuated by the wide tan face; a wiry, not unattractive man who had weighed the same one hundred fifty pounds since he was eighteen. His daily uniform was a pair of khaki shorts and a white tee shirt, a tan fishing cap with embroidered crossed anchors and an extended bill, and usually an unfiltered Camel dangling from his lower lip.

"You'll have to go into Tallahassee soon to find me a typewriter," said Mother Sauls. "I can't keep this up in longhand. It's going to be very lengthy." She was fanning herself with a huge paper fan with a color picture of a peaches-and-cream Jesus printed on one side and some Scripture verses on the other. Bobby watched as she slowly, almost imperceptibly moved the fan back and forth. He stirred from his reverie.

"Why do you want to write it all down?" he asked. There were some birds working the water a half mile out, but there were no flying fish, and it was starting to get dark.

"I want to remember everything," she said. "I've had an interesting life. It'll be a good story. Maybe the movies will want it. It'll have everything—romance, sex, deceit." She stopped the fan in midstroke and looked at him. She was fat, and the flesh on the backside of her arms waved loosely when she started the fan again. She was covered with brown splotches from so many years in that sun, but Bobby saw her slender and smooth, stretching to hang clothes on a line in a wind off the Gulf. He could not remember when that had been—or if it had happened at all. Bobby flexed his aching knees and put his feet up on a milk crate in front of his chair.

"Your papers will be full of fish," he said. "And hot days, and the smell of oyster shells in the yard. You've forgotten how they smell because you've always known it."

"I haven't forgotten," said Mother Sauls. "That will be

in there, but there's more, too." She didn't say what else there was, and Bobby started thinking about flying fish again—how they would likely come in waves from the Gulf in long, successive leaps until they filled the yard.

"I like the smell," Mother Sauls said after a long time.

Besides being his wife, she was also his first cousin. They had known each other all their lives, growing up together there on the coast, the offspring of cousins in a matrimonial tradition begun two generations before theirs in an isolated area where the pickings for mates were slim—a tradition that was now looked on with pride for the mark it produced. They both carried that sign of their parents' incest, an extra little finger on the right hand, as did their grandson, Junior, their granddaughter, Linda, and her husband, Ronnie. None of them had lived more than forty miles from where they were now.

Bobby had spent thirty-five years in the oyster boats on Apalachee Bay until his knees gave out from standing flexed for ten hours a day. Now Ronnie at twenty-four was in the boats, and he in turn took fifteen-year-old Junior out with him in the summer.

"Junior tells me Ronnie says he'll drown the baby if it ain't got the finger," Bobby said to Mother, as he watched a tern bullet down the beach just above the surf line in the ashy light. When he said it, his voice startled him; he couldn't remember whether Junior had really told him or he had made it up himself out of the tangible heat. He rubbed his hand on his pants leg.

"I know," Mother Sauls said. "Linda was in the store this afternoon. Ronnie's getting crazy as shit about this baby. He's convinced now it ain't his. He's really scared her. You need to talk to him."

"I can't," Bobby said. "I don't like him."

"What's that got to do with it?"

"He doesn't listen. He's crazy."

"He might do it," said Mother Sauls.

"He will do it," Bobby said. "But what if it really is his, but something happens and it's born without the finger anyway? What then?"

"He'll drown it, I reckon," said Mother Sauls.

"It's possible it could be born without and still be his," Bobby said.

"Not likely. It hasn't happened yet. You need to talk to him to slow him down a little. It won't be long now until she has it, and she's really in no shape to go through having a baby wondering if her husband's going to drown it like the runt in some litter."

"There's phosphorus in the surf tonight," Bobby said. "You can see it when it breaks. Look there."

"I see it," said Mother Sauls. "You talk to him tomorrow when he comes back from the bay."

Bobby woke in the night to the moon on the Gulf and a light breeze off the water blowing the thin white curtains of the bedroom window. Mother Sauls was snoring in the next bed. Bobby watched the curtains float and fall on the moonlight awhile, and then he got up and lit a cigarette, put on his tan fisherman's cap with the crossed anchors on it, and went out to the porch. It was cooler there, and the moonlight was an incandescent crackling highway on the water, like the coquina road out in front of the cottages had been before they paved it—luminescent even on the darkest nights.

He had been dreaming about the woman on the ice

route. He had been in his twenties when he ran the route—
before he went into the oyster boats—and they had been
lovers. Bobby often thought of her. Sometimes he dreamed
of her, and sometimes she appeared in his waking thoughts;
she was one of the only things in his life he was now
certain had really happened. For a long time, in the oyster
boats, after their brief affair had ended, he was able to
keep her from his mind because he was strong and could
focus his attention down the long-handled tongs that pulled
the oysters from the bottom of the bay. He would put his
mind down the tongs and lift the oysters with his thoughts.
But when he left the boats and began spending his days
on the porch by the Gulf, she returned to drift in and out
among the flying fish and rolling porpoises of his ram-
blings. In his chair on the porch, Bobby sat and watched
the jumping path of moonlight.

He heard a screen door slap. He could tell by the sound
that it was at Ronnie and Linda's place. Their door always had three slaps to it—one initial loud one and two
diminishing bounces. It was Ronnie coming for Junior to
go out in the oyster boats. Bobby could hear his heavy,
loose steps coming toward the cottage through the dry,
burned grass, and in a minute Ronnie appeared at the
porch door and quietly let himself in, making certain not
to let the screen door slap there. Bobby let him come all
the way in before speaking.

"You don't have to worry," Bobby said. "You won't
wake anybody here. We're all deaf, except Junior."

"I'm not worried. I knew you'd be up. Don't you ever
sleep anymore?" He came onto the porch and stood in
front of Bobby. He was nearly as tall as Ike but carried
much less weight, though he had the makings of a good

beer belly. He was clean-shaven and really quite hand-some, Bobby thought, for an oysterman.

"An old man doesn't need to sleep," Bobby said. "Besides, something might happen he can't afford to miss. I'll go get Junior." He didn't want to have to talk to Ronnie about the baby. He started to get up, but Ronnie stepped over and held him down with a gentle push of his hand.

"There's time," Ronnie said. "I came early because I knew you'd be up."

"Why?" Bobby asked. He looked up at Ronnie and was suddenly afraid, and he realized he had been afraid of Ronnie for a long time, but not just because of his size and strength. Ike was bigger and stronger, and he wasn't afraid of Ike. It was, he realized, because of Ronnie's perseverance that he was dangerous and to be feared. He was like that on the boats. He worked silently and with great efficiency and never gave up. When he got an idea, he wouldn't let go of it until he killed it one way or another. He reminded Bobby of the big male blue crabs they found in the channels off the river, in the saw grass and flats of the bay: when disturbed, they would grab and hold on with their great claw, even past death.

But then Ronnie softened right in front of him. He let go of Bobby's shoulder and sat down cross-legged on the porch floor in front of him. "Look, old man," Ronnie said, "I got to find out if this baby is really mine. I got suspicions that are driving me crazy. You've got to help me."

"What can I do?" Bobby asked.

"Find out from Linda," Ronnie said.

"You think she's going to tell me she's been screwing with another man?"

"She might," Ronnie said, "if it's bothering her bad enough."

"What does she tell you?"

"She swears it's mine, of course."

"Then it is. Why don't you believe her?"

"I just got a feeling," Ronnie said. "I'll drown it if it ain't mine."

"So I hear," Bobby said. "But suppose it is yours and it's still born without the finger. That's possible, you know."

"Look," Ronnie said, shaking a fist at Bobby, then self-consciously withdrawing it. "You've got it. I've got it. Mother, Linda, and Junior's got it. If this kid don't have it, it ain't mine. That's all there is to it. Now I wish you'd talk to her and find out for sure."

"I'll try," Bobby said, but he knew he wouldn't.

Ronnie stood again. "Find out," he said. He had thick arms, red arms from the oystering, which showed no muscle definition except in the forearms. "I think it's Ike's," he said, "and I think it's still going on. He's just waiting for it to be born so he can start up again. I'm in the boats all day, you know."

"Not Ike," Bobby said. "Maybe one of the others, but not Ike. He's somewheres else, thinking about the prediction, and he ain't interested in no pregnant woman."

Ronnie laughed. "Ain't nobody thinking about that prediction but you," he said. "That's not what he stayed around for."

"Watch out for Ike," Bobby said. "He ain't no dumb fisherman."

"Meaning I am?" said Ronnie.

"Meaning don't be saying things you don't know for sure, Ronnie." Bobby got up from the chair and started into the kitchen. "I'm going to make some coffee," he said. "You want some?"

"Just try to find out," Ronnie repeated. "Where's that damn Junior? We have to get going."

Bobby had made his way into the kitchen, where he could see the rose glow beginning out over the eastern part of the Gulf. He stood at the counter, making coffee the way the dark-haired woman on the ice route had made it, long ago.

THREE

The afternoon Mr. Wilkes arrived at the cottages lugging the pillowcase that contained the bones of his infant son, Psychic Ike was reading Linda's fortune in the cards under a big canvas beach umbrella set up out in the long, vee-shaped yard. Linda listened to Ike describe the long, happy life her baby was going to have, that it was going to be a girl and move away from the coast, that she would marry rich—everything but whether or not she would have the extra little finger on her right hand. Bobby sat under the umbrella with them, occasionally dozing or scanning the flat water and horizon while he drank a beer. Ike saw Wilkes first, and if he knew anything then, he didn't say it. Weeks later, Bobby wondered why Ike hadn't known right away what Wilkes was carrying and what it all meant, because Bobby continued to believe in Ike's powers long after even Ike had said they didn't really exist.

"We've finally got a customer," Ike said, nodding in

the direction of the stranger and Mother Sauls making their way through the heat between the cottages. The sunlight shot off the white siding, and Bobby lost them for a moment.

Linda turned and looked and said, "Appears to be alone too." The stranger was carrying a suitcase in one hand; in the other he had the pillowcase, which swung along and brushed against his leg. Mother Sauls waved happily to the little group under the umbrella and took the man into the third cottage back from the beach. Every few seconds they could see her throw open another window and talk to the man at the same time, but they couldn't hear what she was saying.

"He's pretty young," Linda said. "I wonder what he's doing out here by himself." She turned back, and Bobby was struck by how beautiful her pregnancy had made her. Her face was plump and pink, but she had really gained little excess weight. She looked healthier than he had ever seen her. And happy when she smiled. She had long, honey-blond hair pulled back in a ponytail; the loose strands waved around her ears. Best of all were her lovely, even teeth, which shone when she smiled. Bobby loved her teeth, and he hoped the baby would have them too. He hoped Ronnie would not have to drown the baby.

"He's probably a salesman or something," Bobby said.

"He looks like a wimp," Ike said. "All guys like him are wimps." He looked at Linda and smiled. "Ain't he a wimp, Linda?"

"Oh, stop it, you big asshole," Linda said. "You don't know anything about him. He's probably very nice."

"He's a wimp, and I'm gonna kick his ass," Ike said.

"Oh, shut up," said Linda. Bobby laughed and took

another beer out of the cooler at his feet. He watched as Mother Sauls came out of the stranger's cottage and started across the grass to their gathering. Ike began picking up the cards.

"Who is it?" Bobby asked, as Mother Sauls came up, smiling.

"His name is Wilkes," said Mother Sauls, "and he's from Dothan. He says he's going to stay about a month. He paid me for it in advance." She stood with her arms folded and smiled at each of them in turn as if her head were being pulled along that arc by a slow, smooth-running motor. "He builds swimming pools," she added.

"Any wife?" Linda asked.

"Why do you want to know?" said Mother Sauls.

"Just curious," Linda answered. "He looks like he should have a wife."

"Maybe he should," said Mother Sauls. "But he didn't mention it, and I didn't ask. And don't you either."

"I won't, Grandma, jeez," Linda said.

"Well, I'm going back to get some cold beer from the store," said Mother Sauls. "I've invited him to come out and have a beer with us after he washes up a little. Bobby, you get us a couple more lawn chairs. There's some on the porch of that cottage over there, I think. I'll be right back. If he comes out while I'm gone, y'all be nice to him."

"We will, Grandma, jeez," Linda said.

"I'm gonna kick his butt," Ike growled, so Mother Sauls could hear him. She veered around in midstride as if his words had physically yanked her and came back to the umbrella. "Listen, Ike, you big gorilla," she said, "you mind your manners. Ain't nobody scared of you."

"Yes, ma'am." Ike smiled.

Bobby watched her stride back off across the grass in the awful heat and thought how well she still moved. She walked with a quickness and authority he lacked. She was tough and in charge. "I'll get the chairs," he said, and went off to the empty cottage Mother Sauls had pointed out.

He didn't find the chairs on the porch where she said they'd be. Since they never locked any of the cottages, he pushed open the kitchen door and went into the empty house. In the kitchen he was met by the heavy, pungent smell of rotting fish. Bobby at first thought it might be something left behind by some of the guests, maybe by some of Ike's biker friends. But then he remembered which cottage it was and why they had closed it off, and he knew no one had stayed there in a very long time. Then he thought perhaps Junior had been using the place to clean the fish he caught down in the surf. Bobby checked, but found nothing in the shut-down refrigerator or in the sink. Anyway, the smell was too great to have been just leftover fish. The air in the cottage was yellow and so thick he could taste it, but the smell was not in the kitchen.

He found what it was in the living room There were hundreds of dead flying fish covering the floor and piled in mounds on the furniture. Most of their bodies were rotted away. But their transparent fin wings—in which there were now hundreds of rainbows dryly glistening— lay intact. Bobby stood in the stinking heat of the room a long time, unable to move, staring at the bodies of the flying fish and the incredible shimmering pattern of rainbows reflected on the walls, as dusty sunlight passed through the curtainless windows. Then, hearing Mother Sauls calling his name as if from the other end of the world, he turned his back on the fish, found two metal folding chairs propped against the wall, and carried them back out through the kitchen and the porch into the sun between the cottages.

The unfiltered sunlight was dazzling after the dank, yellow stuffiness of the cottage, and partly because of that, Bobby stumbled halfway to the umbrella and went to his knees, dropping the chairs in a long clatter. Going down, he was not thinking of the flying fish, but of the awful, independent mortality of his knees as things apart from the rest of his body, and of the scorched, malevolent sky that stretched overhead. Psychic Ike saw him fall and was quick to help him up. Bobby let him, felt himself coming up from the crisp grass as if without substance in Ike's unequivocal grip. But he could not bring himself to tell Ike about the flying fish because it had been too flat and sad to see them in the living room of the cottage. It was nothing like he had imagined. When he got to his feet, he was crying, and Ike wiped his tears with a big blue handkerchief as if he were wiping away the sweat and sand. Mother Sauls helped Ike get Bobby back in the shade of the umbrella, and Ike went back for the fallen chairs.

Mother Sauls placed Bobby in one of the chairs and looked deep into his eyes. "Are you all right?" she asked. His eyes roved over the lines of her face and into the sagging flesh of her jaws. "Yes," he answered. "Yes, I'm all right now. It's the heat." He felt the others were embarrassed for him so he did not look at them, but rather held out his hand to Wilkes, who stood nearby holding a beer can. "I'm Bobby Sauls," he said. What he wanted to say was "There's a roomful of flying fish over there I know nothing about," but what came out was "Sorry about the heat." He tried to look Wilkes in the eye anyway. The eyes were very pleasant and intelligent.

"It's all right," Wilkes said. "I'm used to it." Bobby saw the beginnings of a smile on Wilkes's face, but it never came and Bobby looked away.

"Of course you are," said Mother Sauls. "You're nothing like those thick-blooded Yankees we get. They get thick blood from having to live in that damn cold, and then they come down here and complain about the heat because their blood's too thick, and then they air-condition the shit out of everything, and it ends up being just like what they left to get away from."

"I guess that's it," Wilkes said. "By the way, thanks for the beer." He felt for one of the lawn chairs behind him and sat down.

Bobby looked out at the Gulf. "It's good beer," he said. "It's Miller. We get a truckload of it every week, and we do our best to finish it off before the next truck comes. And then we all go line up down at the beach and piss it into the Gulf." He was still looking out at the hot, flat water, but then he turned to Ike and said, "They came, and I missed them."

"What?"

"I'll tell you later," Bobby said. "But it wasn't quite like I pictured it."

"Are you sure you're all right?" Ike said. "Maybe you ought to go lie down."

"I'm really fine," Bobby said. "I just got a little woozy there. It was those damn flying fish."

"Don't worry, Mr. Wilkes," said Mother Sauls. "He's old, but he's harmless. I remember when he wasn't old. In fact, he was quite the rake when he was an ice-man."

"That's right. She remembers everything," Bobby said. "Ask her. She never forgets anything. She writes it all down." His head was swimming, and he leaned down between his knees and took a deep breath, which made him feel better.

Mother Sauls smiled. "He's right. I have a wonderful memory, thank God; that's why I'm able to write it all down. I haven't forgotten a thing."

"She's like a goddamn swordfish," Bobby said. "Where's the damn beer?"

"Granddad, that doesn't make sense," Linda said uneasily.

"No? What did I say that didn't make sense?"

"You said grandmother was like a swordfish. That doesn't make any sense."

"Well, I didn't mean swordfish, exactly. I meant sword. She's more like a sword."

"Goddamn drunk." Ike laughed. "Here, have another beer." He reached into the cooler at his feet, pulled out a can, and popped it for Bobby. "Here," he said. "Shut up and drink."

Bobby took the cold can from Ike and tilted his head back so he was looking at the inside of the big umbrella. It was striped like a circus tent, and cheerful. He felt better looking at it. A long silence occupied the little group until Ike finally opened another can of beer with a long hissing pop.

Wilkes stood, holding his own empty beer can. "Well,"

he said. "Thanks for the beer. I think I'll go unpack and take a little rest. That was a long drive from Dothan."

Bobby looked up at him. Wilkes had the kind of olive skin that would tan deeply and easily in this sun. He was lean and graceful and soft-spoken, and Bobby liked him. "You play cards, Mr. Wilkes?" Bobby asked.

Wilkes smiled. "A little gin rummy."

Bobby shook his head. "Nope," he said, "I was thinking more of canasta. Nobody around here can play canasta."

"Maybe you can teach me," Wilkes said, "once I get settled."

"You just go right ahead, Mr. Wilkes," Mother Sauls said. "I'll be bringing you over a fan later. I know you'll be needing one. If there's anything else, just let me know."

"Thank you," said Wilkes, and he started to leave the tent.

"Say, Mr. Wilkes," Linda said, "Psychic Ike here tells fortunes. Why don't you let him tell yours?"

"I don't think so." Wilkes smiled. "Maybe some other time. I really don't believe in that, I guess."

"Me neither," Linda said. "But Ike's pretty entertaining. It's something to do anyway."

Wilkes stood looking at them. Bobby looked down the vee of cottages to the Gulf. On the horizon there was a cloud in the shape of a butterfly with a double set of wings, moving very slowly from east to west. It was the first cloud Bobby had seen in more than a week. Closer in, above the cloud and moving in the same direction, was a small airplane with sunlight flashing from its nearest wing. "Hey, Ike," Bobby said, pointing to the spot out over the Gulf, "is that plane going to crash here?"

"No way," Ike said.

"See, Mr. Wilkes," Bobby said. "Ike knows the future. He's the best there is."

Ike had his Harley-Davidson spread out in pieces again on an olive green canvas tarp outside the porch of his cottage. It was after ten o'clock at night, and he worked under a shop light he had hanging from a limb of the pine that stood near his back door. A thick yellow extension cord trailed down out of the tree and back into the screen porch.

Bobby sat outside the circle of white light in a lawn chair and watched Ike work. He was holding a can of bug spray that Ike occasionally called for, and when he did, Bobby would toss it to him in a high, end-over-end arc. Ike would spray his bare, sweating torso and great arms and toss the can back to Bobby in the same way. Ike was cleaning some of the parts of the bike with kerosene, using a small, stiff paintbrush. Most of the time he sat on the canvas with his legs out in front of him, his enormous belly falling between his legs, nearly touching the canvas.

From his own cottage Bobby had seen the little circle of light and the hovering cloud of moths at the other end of the yard. He walked over intending to tell Ike about finding the flying fish in the empty house. But as he thought about it, crossing the dark space between the cottages, he was afraid they had not been there at all. In the black, cool clarity of the night, with the constellations poked into the sky above and Ike's surreal but friendly circle of light ahead, Bobby understood that if the others went into the cottage they would find nothing there but dusty furniture. Bobby did not understand what he had seen, but he didn't want Ike to think him any more of a fool than he probably already did.

Ike was working slowly and meticulously, cleaning the same parts he had cleaned only two days before. The black frame of the bike stood denuded outside the circle of light, and Bobby sat fascinated with its clean, angular simplicity and listened to the cicadas in the trees and the crickets in the palmettos.

"Friend of mine once told me a long time ago that all crickets everywhere in the world are chirping the same rhythm at the same time," Bobby said. "I believed him a long time too; I believed everything he said."

"Goddamn mosquitoes," Ike swore, flailing at the air. "They're big as fucking trucks. How come they don't get you?"

"They used to," Bobby said. "When I was young, they wouldn't leave me alone. I guess I'm too old now and they don't want anything to do with me. Maybe I don't have any blood left."

"How long've you been here?" Ike asked, without looking up from the part he was working on.

"All my life," Bobby answered. "Well, not right here, but close by. We got this place right after the war. Mother Sauls had saved money for years. Everything I got in the Civilian Conservation Corps, she saved."

Ike looked up. "You were in the CCC?"

"Yeah," Bobby said. "Not too far from here. We built the park up at Torrea, at the Georgia border, during the depression. Like everything else, the oyster business fell apart, and I had to do something. That was just for a little while, and then I went back into the boats. Worked my ass off in those oyster boats."

"So you got this place?"

"Yeah, and Mother ran it while I did the oystering, and then my knees gave out, and I quit. It keeps us going. Every now and then we fill the place up."

Ike nodded and looked at Bobby a long time. "Nothing's really going to happen here, you know. There's not going to be any great revelation, or anything. I want to tell you that."

"I know," Bobby said. "Nothing ever happens here."

"So why do you keep after it?"

"I don't know. Maybe because everything's been the same here for fifty years. Sometimes I believe its going to happen, sometimes not. Tomorrow I might believe it again; it's just that right now, I don't."

"I'm telling you, it's all bullshit," Ike said. "I made it all up. I don't know what's going to happen five minutes from now."

"That's all right," Bobby said. "You don't know everything. Maybe you're right and don't know it. About the prediction, I mean."

"That's the craziest logic I've ever heard," Ike said. "You're one crazy old man, Bobby."

"It's good to have something to believe in," Bobby said. "Let's keep doing it."

"Even with knowing I made it all up?"

"Especially with that," Bobby said. "When you've been around as long as I have, you'll know it doesn't make any difference what you believe in, just so you believe in something."

Ike picked up the paintbrush again and went back to

cleaning the parts. There were moths dancing wildly around his hair, descending in a column from the light in the tree. Bobby looked up. There were great dark shadows from the tree's lower limbs and a few needles in the sparse upper reaches silhouetted against the stars. "I bet you I'm older than that tree," he said.

Ike looked up too. "No," he said. "I know about trees. That tree's more than eighty years old. Look at the size of it."

"Fifty," Bobby said. "Not a year more. They grow like crazy around here. You don't know nothing."

"Maybe," Ike said. He went back to work.

Bobby rubbed his hands back and forth on the smooth, tubular aluminum arms of the lawn chair and thought about the flying fish he had seen piled up in the empty cottage, how their wings had made rainbows on the walls, the same kind of rainbows he remembered making when he was a child by holding his eyes nearly closed and peering out at a sunlit window. The light was broken up into the spectrum by his lashes, and it was just that way with the light coming through the flying fish wings. It was like remembering a dream, maybe even someone else's dream.

Bobby looked at Ike bent into his work, his ponderous belly quivering when he moved the paintbrush, the moths circling his hair. He tried to put into words why he did care so much about the prediction. Maybe it was just that after all this time he thought there'd be something more. This couldn't be all there was. "I've been wondering all my life what we're doing here," he said. "I really have."

Ike looked up and smiled. "I'm working on my Harley," he said. "I don't know what the hell you're doing here."

"Sometimes I think I'm losing my mind," Bobby said.

On the way back to his own cottage through the warm, surrounding dark, Bobby saw the red glow of a cigarette ash on Linda and Ronnie's screen porch, and around it, Ronnie's softly illuminated, expressionless death mask. But he did not stop.

Her name was Mary, and she had lived at the mouth of the St. Marks River with her fisherman husband. They had a small grocery and bait store attached to the front of their house. When he was twenty-one, Bobby used to deliver two fifty-pound blocks of ice there every Tuesday and Thursday morning on his coastal ice route. He made his delivery early—before the sun had fully risen—but after her husband had left for his day of fishing. She would have fresh coffee for him, and they would sit in the kitchen and talk. It was weeks before anything happened.

At first, because she was so beautiful, he had been ashamed to have her see his extra finger and tried to keep that hand hidden from her when he brought in the big blocks of ice. But when she found it, when they were lovers, she often held it up before her face to admire it— caress it, kiss it, laugh and cry about it.

The finger became the focus of a game for them in the salty mornings of her room overlooking the brown, undulating marsh grass at the mouth of the St. Marks River. When he learned the depth of her fascination for his little deformity, he would withhold it from her until they made love in the room where it was always morning and the light was dim and new and there was always the smell of coffee mingling with that of the warm, wet marsh and her own mustiness. Then she would find it, under a pillow, or lost in her hair, and she would bring it to her face and address it as a person or some valued pet.

"Will you live with Bobby always?" she would ask, and, "Do you love me, or are you going to leave me too?"

Bobby would speak in a high voice, pretending to be the finger. "Where can I go?" he would say. "I'm just a stepchild, tied up to this dumb fucker next to me. Of course I'll stay."

And then he discovered her own hands, with the cord-like veins that so belied the frailty of her body. He would hold them as long as he could while the sun rose and grew hot. And because of the winding prominence of those veins, he came to believe that she was much stronger than he, that her strength had pressed them to the surface. And he loved her more because he was not strong. Every morning when he left her house to continue his route, there would be a breeze coming off the Gulf, up the flat, black-water mouth of the river and across the marsh grass. And he would remember that at that moment his young wife was hanging clothes on a line between two pines in the same wind in the dirt and palmetto yard of their own place, some twenty miles up the coast; remember that every morning those clothes smelling of salt and sun would be laid out for him on their bed—and he would promise himself he wasn't coming back to this woman on the river.

Bobby was at his place on the porch by the Gulf. He held his right hand up to the moon, blocked its light with his two little fingers, then looked for the glow through the thin web of skin that separated and connected them. It was like looking through an extra-thick piece of wax paper. He held his finger up to the moon and thought about Mother Sauls writing down her life, inside the living room under the floor lamp. He wondered what she would say about his affair when she got to that part of her life. He knew she knew, though they had never once talked about it—she had punished and controlled him with that silence for fifty years. He wondered also how she was treating the finger in her writing: how often it was mentioned, what status it held. To Bobby it had once been a monument to passion, but now it was just another relic he carried around, like his arms and legs, his little tan fishing cap, his thick brown belt. It was still, however, more than anything else except the woman on the ice route, the thing that held him to Mother Sauls.

Bobby heard Mother Sauls cough and shift her position in the chair. Without looking, he could picture the scene: the conical shape of the light from the lamp and the heavy shadows the chair made on the pine floor; Mother Sauls in her pink shorts and white sleeveless blouse, which, except for the color, was like all the others she owned; the clipboard with a yellow legal pad held in her lap while she scribbled away with the stub of a pencil. When she found out about Mary, she very quietly let him know, and he never went back. He did not know how long he would have gone back had she not found out. Maybe if they'd had even one fight about it in these fifty years he wouldn't still be carrying it. Maybe he would have been able to let go.

He finally pulled his hand down from the moon and rose from his chair, intending to tell Mother about the roomful of dead flying fish he had found several days before. But Junior popped out of the hot darkness like a cork and pressed his face against the screen.

"Go to bed," Bobby said to the face that threatened to strain itself through the wire mesh. "You have to work in the morning."

Junior pulled open the door instead of going through it and stepped lightly onto the porch.

"There's something weird going on at Wilkes's place," he said.

"In what way?" Bobby said.

"He's got bones spread out all over the floor," Junior said. "I saw them."

"Bones? You saw them?"

"Yes, Granddad."

"How? Did he show them to you?"

"Not exactly. I could see them through the window."

"You were looking through the window? Junior, some-body's going to shoot you for that one day, boy. What the hell were you doing looking in the man's window?"

Bobby sensed for a moment the smell of rain on the air, and he wanted to close his eyes and follow the scent, even if it was unreal, but there was no shaking Junior when he had news.

"I just wanted to see what he was doing," Junior said. "We never see him, you know. I just wanted to know what he was doing in there by himself all the time, so I crawled up to the window."

"You're lucky he didn't blow your head off," Bobby said, easing back into his seat. Junior pulled up another of the porch chairs so he was right in front of Bobby.

"You should be glad I looked," Junior said. "The man's got a skeleton in there, Granddad."

"So what?"

"So, what's he doing with a skeleton in one of our cottages? He had all the bones laid out according to size and shape on the floor, and he was just sitting there looking at them."

"What kind of skeleton was it?"

"What do you mean? It was bones," Junior said.

"No, dummy. Was it some kind of animal, maybe? He might be some kind of animal scientist or something."

"I don't know," Junior said. "It was all in pieces, and they were all small. And he ain't no scientist, either. Grandma says he builds pools."

"That's right," Bobby said. "I forgot about that."

"So, what are you going to do?" Junior asked, his face only a few inches from Bobby's.

"I'm going to bed," Bobby said. "Right after you do. I thought you were already inside. I'll tell Ike about it in the morning, and we'll decide what to do. Now, go to bed."

Junior got up and started into the kitchen. "Wilkes is a weird guy, Granddad. I'm telling you."

"Thanks," Bobby said.

In the night Bobby dreamed about German submarines off the coast just like during the blackout days of the war, when black curtains were hung in houses all along the Gulf and they would watch for cruising subs that never came out on the dark water. In his dream a sub did appear, and the captain stood on the bridge and called to

Bobby on the shore in English with a thick German accent.

"Yo, Bobby Sauls," the German called, "are you there?"

Bobby, sitting in his chair on the porch, could vaguely see the outline of the sub against the somewhat lighter black of the sky. "Who wants to know?" he called back.

"We have your son." The German captain laughed. "We're sending him in."

Bobby woke up and listened to Mother Sauls sleeping until it was light, and then he put on his shorts and lit a Camel and went out to tell Ike about Wilkes and the bones. He forgot about the dream when he got into the light of the yard, and he waved to Linda, who was out hanging laundry next to her cottage.

"How do you feel?" Bobby called to her. She looked like Mother Sauls had looked years ago hanging clothes in a wind from the Gulf.

"Fine, Granddad," she answered. "I feel fine, but I'm ready for this to be over. I feel like I've been pregnant forever."

Bobby waved again and hurried on to Ike's place. Linda would be all right, he thought. Even if the baby didn't have the finger. She was tough, and she was good. Loyal and resilient. She knew what it meant to be a Sauls, even if Ronnie didn't. When Linda and Junior's father died, and their mother deserted them, leaving the infant Junior wrapped in newspaper on Bobby and Mother's porch, Linda did her best to fill that void. She doted on Junior and later fought for him in school when kids teased him about the finger. Bobby remembered when Junior had been sick with meningitis the summer he was nine. Linda had ridden with Junior's head in her lap all the way to the hospital in Tallahassee, stroking the boy's hair and whispering to him. She stayed awake holding his hand all night, until he was out of danger. Bobby knew about good because it was so rare—that made it easy to spot if you knew how, but not everybody knew how. He still hadn't made up his mind about Ike. Ike could still go either way, Bobby thought. He smelled coffee coming from Ike's kitchen and remembered he hadn't had his yet.

Ike was in the front room, straightening out his psychic and séance stuff. He had astrological charts on the wall and several decks of cards on a small round table covered with a long, draping black cloth. The table was placed in the exact center of the room. There were many candles in various kinds of holders, either scattered or arranged about the room—Bobby couldn't tell which. He looked out the front window at the braced back of Ike's huge sign, which cast a generous patch of early morning shade.

"You got any coffee?" Bobby asked.

"Goddamn," Ike said. "You went right past it in the kitchen. Help yourself."

"It's just that I haven't had mine yet," Bobby said. "And I have something to tell you. I'm not bothering you, am I?"

"Oh, no," Psychic Ike said, dusting a candle-laden shelf with a red bandanna. "But it better not be another flying fish story."

"It's not," Bobby said. "You want some coffee?"

"No," Ike said. "I only made it because I knew you'd be coming over."

"Thanks," Bobby said. "You really do know what's going to happen next, don't you?"

"With you, I do," said Ike.

Bobby went into the kitchen and poured himself a big mug, left it black, and went back to join Ike. He found him sitting on the worn red Naugahyde sofa, shirtless and wearing jeans and black motorcycle boots, which he had propped on a wooden straight-backed chair in front of the sofa. Ike glared at Bobby.

"You ought to do something about this furniture, old man," Ike said. "I keep sticking to this fucking stuff. I have to peel myself off this goddamn sofa every time I sit here."

"So, don't sit there," Bobby said, taking one of the chairs at the table. "Besides, that's Mother Sauls's department."

"Well, tell her to get some new shit, man. Come on, what's on your feeble little mind this morning. I've got a customer coming in at nine o'clock, so hurry up."

"Junior tells me Wilkes has a skeleton in his place," Bobby said.

"A skeleton?"

"Yeah. Junior says he saw the bones spread out all over the floor."

"Maybe the guy just had barbecue, man. Come on."

"No," Bobby said. "Junior says it's a skeleton."

"I wonder what he's doing messing with a skeleton," Ike said.

"You're supposed to know," Bobby said. "That's why I came to you."

"Shit, man," Ike bellowed. "I told you I can't even tell if the sun's coming up tomorrow. I don't know what the fuck he's doing with a skeleton."

"We'd better find out," Bobby said.

"So ask him," Ike said. "Look, man, I've got to get

ready. This chick's loaded, and she think's I can talk to her dead old man. This is a big one."

"I can't ask him," Bobby said. "I don't want him to know we were sneaking around and found out."

"So, you're saying it's better to sneak around and find out what he's doing rather than him thinking you are."

"Yes," Bobby said. "That's it. What should we do?"

Ike thought for a minute. "Look," he said, "when I get done with this chick, I'll come get you. Then I'll get Wilkes to come over here and look at all this shit and maybe give him a free reading, and you hop in there and see what he's up to."

"Good," Bobby said. "Great."

"All right," Ike said. "We'll spy on the little bastard. But right now, get the fuck out of here. I don't want you blowing this one for me. I'll come find you when I'm done. Don't do anything without me."

"I won't," Bobby said. "Thanks." He got up and put the coffee mug on the table with the black cloth on it. "Not there, old man," Ike said. "Take it in the kitchen and put it in the fucking sink."

"Sorry," Bobby said.

After he went out the screen door at the back of the cottage, he stood in the already hot sun for a moment, thinking of what to do next. When he saw Linda still at her clothesline, he started for her house to wait for Psychic Ike.

Ike came to the store around noon to get him. Bobby was drinking a beer, watching Mother Sauls put away stock from a truck that had delivered that morning. He had

been watching her a long time, but they hadn't said anything to each other in over an hour. Ike came in wearing
his jeans and a sleeveless tee shirt, under which his belly
swelled like a watermelon. "Come on," he said to Bobby.
"Let's get started." Bobby could read Ike's God Forgives
tattoo through the shirt.

Mother Sauls was stocking the shelf with Vienna sausages when she stopped what she was doing right in the
middle. She turned to glare at Ike and Bobby. "What are
you two hooligans up to?" she said.

"Nothing, ma'am." Ike smiled. "It's just a little scheme
of Bobby's. I won't let him get in any trouble, though."

"See that you don't," she said, turning back to the Vienna sausage. "I reckon between the two of you, you might
be able to keep from tearing up the place or getting killed.
I'm counting on you, Ike, to keep Bobby out of trouble—
God, that's like hiring the fox to watch the chickens—
but he does irresponsible, sneaky things when I've got my
back turned."

"We'll be good, Ma," Ike said.

Bobby got out of the chair and tried to straighten his
aching knees. "It takes a while to get started sometimes,"
he complained to Ike. "I'll be back later, Mother."

"Come on,'" Ike said.

Outside, Ike confronted Bobby. "You act like you got
to get permission from that old woman to breathe," he
said. "Has it always been that way, or did you just get
pussy-whipped recently?"

"It's nothing," Bobby said. "We've just been together a
long time. I don't really listen to her anyway." Ike continued to look at him, smiling his big, hairy smile. "I'll tell
you about it sometime," Bobby said.

"Look," Ike said. "You hang out around here. I'll go roust out Wilkes. When you see us go by you've got fifteen minutes to check the place out, no more. I maybe could distract him a half hour, but to be safe, you've got fifteen minutes. OK?"

"OK," Bobby said.

"All right, you wait here." Ike went up to Wilkes's door and knocked. In a few seconds Wilkes met him outside. After they'd talked for a minute, Wilkes closed his front door, and they started back across the yard. Bobby felt very conspicuous standing outside the store for no reason, so he waved to Wilkes and Ike and ducked back inside the store to watch through the screen door as they passed. Ike was talking a mile a minute, and Wilkes was looking straight ahead.

"What the hell are you doing?" said Mother Sauls.

Bobby turned away from the door. "Nothing," he said. "I came back in for a can of those Vienna sausages. Let me have one."

Mother Sauls was on the ladder against the shelves, and she reached over and got him a can. "Here," she said. "You're acting crazy."

"I am crazy," Bobby said. "But that's because I'm a hundred and twenty years old." He took the can and went back outside, then hurried as fast as his bad knees would take him over to Wilkes's cottage, went around to the porch side facing the Gulf, and let himself in. First he opened the can of sausages, and then he started looking through the house.

Wilkes had apparently brought very little with him, but in the living room Bobby found what he was hunting for. On the coffee table was a long pasteboard box, the kind canned vegetables were delivered in, and in it was what appeared to be a partly assembled skeleton of a very small human. Next to the box on the table was a roll of thin-gauge wire, some cutters, and a hand-operated drill with a tiny bit. Bobby looked at the contents of the box and slowly chewed one of the sausages. When he finished it, he wiped his hands on his shorts and picked up the white pillowcase laying under the table. It contained loose bones and a small human skull. Wilkes was assembling the skeleton with bits of wire right there in the living room. Bobby put the pillowcase back and sat down on the sofa. It was like finding the dead flying fish in the other cottage. He would be afraid to tell Ike what he had found because it probably wasn't there. But *Junior* had seen the bones. That's why he was here in the first place! He would tell Ike, and together they would decide what Wilkes was doing with a skeleton. Maybe he would even tell Ike about the flying fish in the cottage.

Bobby sat back in the sofa and had another Vienna sausage while looking at the little leg bones Wilkes had assembled in the box. They were hardly bigger than rabbit bones. He heard a screen door slap across the yard and remembered he was supposed to be gone when Ike brought Wilkes back. Bobby hurried out to the porch and quietly let himself out. He could hear Ike and Wilkes coming across the yard. Ike was laughing in his best big, round biker tones.

Bobby walked down to his own cottage and took his usual seat, to wait for Ike. They had not determined where to meet, but Bobby knew Ike would come.

The Gulf was churning more than usual, and there were more clouds. But nothing indicated rain. Bobby closed his eyes and listened to the crickets and cicadas in the pines and palmettos. Their drone was the sound of the sun. He was nearly asleep when Ike climbed onto the porch. Bobby was startled, and his hands went up reflexively in front of him.

"Nodding out on me again, huh?" Ike said.

"Almost," said Bobby. "I could use a nap."

"Well, what did you find out?" Ike was looking at Bobby carefully.

"He definitely has a skeleton in there," Bobby answered. "Just like Junior said. It's very small, like a baby or something."

"You sure it's not some kind of animal?"

"Positive," Bobby said. "I saw the skull. Part of it's in a pillowcase, and he has some of it put together. He's doing it with bits of wire. He drills holes in the bones and wires them together."

"He's wiring the thing back together?"

"Yes," Bobby answered. "Just like some guys build model ships and planes, he's wiring a skeleton together."

"I wonder what the hell for." Ike was sitting in one of the old metal lawn chairs, scratching his beard.

"I think he's some kind of murderer," Bobby said.

"You have to talk to him," Ike said firmly. "It's your place, you talk to him."

"Well, Mother runs it, actually."

"You know what I mean."

"Well, what should I say? Do I ask him why he's putting a skeleton together?"

"I don't know. Play it by ear," Ike said. "You can do it."

"Maybe I'll just invite myself in," Bobby said. "Maybe he'll bring it up."

"Maybe," Ike said. "Say, this is great, isn't it. This might even take your mind off that dumb prediction, huh?"

"No," Bobby said. "I'm still thinking about it."

Instead of going to talk to Wilkes as he had told Psychic Ike he would do, Bobby left the porch after supper, with the sky a transparent purple out over the Gulf, and went to the cottage in which he had found the flying fish. He let himself in through the kitchen door and stood still for a moment, afraid to encounter the spoiled-fish smell again. Closing his eyes, he took a deep breath. The air was thick and musty, but there was no smell of dead fish. Bobby went cautiously into the living room. It was empty but for the furniture. Mother Sauls must have found the fish, Bobby reasoned, and cleaned the place up. Or more likely, he remembered, they had never been there at all.

Just to be sure, he went down the short hall and into the bedroom, and what he saw there made his knees give out again and brought on an attack of dry heaves. The room appeared just as he had found it fifteen years before when his son, Jim—Junior and Linda's father—had put a shotgun in his mouth and blown his head off. The sheets and the braided throw rug on the floor were soaked in blood, and there was spattered blood and bits of flesh on the ceiling and the slats of the venetian blinds at the window. The room was very hot and yellow, and Bobby could smell the blood and the exploded flesh. The shotgun lay on the rug by the bed, but Jim was not there. And in a brief moment of cold clarity that was without pain, like a razor drawn quickly across his belly, in the moment before the tears came and he could no longer think, Bobby was glad about that.

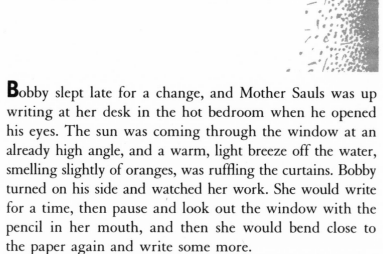

F I V E

Bobby slept late for a change, and Mother Sauls was up writing at her desk in the hot bedroom when he opened his eyes. The sun was coming through the window at an already high angle, and a warm, light breeze off the water, smelling slightly of oranges, was ruffling the curtains. Bobby turned on his side and watched her work. She would write for a time, then pause and look out the window with the pencil in her mouth, and then she would bend close to the paper again and write some more.

"How far along are you?" Bobby asked. He saw her shoulders jump a little at the sound of his voice, but she did not turn around.

"Seven years old," she answered. "The first part is pretty thin. I mean, there are big gaps of time between events I remember, but the more I write, the more I remember. My father is taking me to Wakulla Springs in this part."

"I remember," Bobby said. "You came by our house

4 8

when you got back, and you were very excited. We were living in Grandfather's house then, back up in the woods from Panacea. You couldn't say Wakulla. You said, 'Waka,' or something like that."

Mother Sauls turned in her chair to face him. She was wearing turquoise shorts and a white, sleeveless blouse this morning. "That's right," she said. "Do you really remember that?"

"Sure," Bobby said. "I remember a lot of back then—I just can't remember what happened yesterday." He closed his eyes, recalling the blood he'd seen in the empty cottage, and then he smelled the coffee from the kitchen, and it made his stomach grow active and rumble. "What day is it?" he said.

"Sunday," said Mother Sauls. "Everybody's home today. I thought we'd all get together for dinner this evening. I got some good snapper yesterday I can broil."

Bobby nodded. "Wilkes is wiring together a baby skeleton out of a bunch of bones," he said. "That's what he does over there all day."

Mother Sauls put down her pencil. "So that's what you two were up to yesterday. Spying on Mr. Wilkes. You're supposed to leave the guests alone."

"Did you hear what I said? I said he has a baby's skeleton in a box over there." Bobby got out of bed and pulled on a pair of shorts and his cap. "Don't you think that's kind of strange?"

"I'm sure he has a reason," she said. "He's a nice man."

"He seems to be," Bobby said, "but Jesus Christ, a skeleton? That's a pretty weird thing to be doing on your vacation."

"Maybe it's a hobby of his."

"Baby skeletons are hard to come by," Bobby said. "It's not like fish bones, you know."

"Did you ask him about it? Maybe you ought to ask, if it's going to bother you."

"I will," Bobby said. "I'll ask him after dinner tonight." He stopped on his way to get coffee and looked over her shoulder at the writing on the page. "You're writing down everything you remember?"

"Everything," said Mother Sauls, covering the paper with both hands. "You can't read it. It's private."

Bobby shrugged and headed toward the kitchen. He was pouring himself a cup of coffee when he heard the shouting in the yard. It was Linda's voice. "Stop it, Ronnie," she said. "No, stop it."

Bobby hurried through the living room and into the yard. He could hear Mother Sauls right behind him, coming from the bedroom. Linda was standing outside her cottage, yelling for Ronnie to come back inside. Ronnie was in the middle of the yard, squared off in a fighter's stance against the bigger and much older Psychic Ike. They were circling each other. Out of the corner of his eye Bobby could see Junior coming up at a slow trot from the beach, where he'd been fishing.

"Come back in here, Ronnie," Linda yelled. "You don't have to do this." But Ronnie was paying no attention.

"They're going to kill each other," said Mother Sauls at Bobby's side. "You'd better do something."

"Like hell I will," Bobby said. "Ronnie's got it coming."

Just then Ronnie took a big, looping swing at Ike's jaw and missed. Ike had stepped back from where a short, straight jab might have landed, and Ronnie had got nothing but air. "Son of a bitch," Ronnie said. He circled to

Ike's left, and Ike went with him, his big hands clenched but down and loose at his sides. Ronnie swung again. Ike just moved his head a little this time, and the blow glanced off his ear. "Come on, you big greasy son of a bitch," Ronnie said. "Fight me." Ike said nothing. He stood his ground and turned with Ronnie's circling, his eyes fixed on Ronnie's.

"Come on," Ronnie said again. He was talking, but Bobby could tell he was scared. It was in the quickness of his eyes. But he had talked himself into it, and Bobby knew he wouldn't quit. Linda had stopped yelling. Now she just watched like the others. But she had her hands pressed together over her swollen belly as if to hold everything in, and she was leaning back against the white siding of her cottage. "Linda," Mother Sauls said, loud enough for only Bobby to hear.

Bobby was watching Psychic Ike's hands when it happened. Ronnie came in wildly once more, and Ike's loosely clenched left hand came up with great speed from under his belt and caught Ronnie square on the jaw. It made a nasty sound when it landed, and Bobby quickly remembered some of the other fights he'd seen and how brutal and unlike anything on TV they were. It was almost better to be in one than to watch it, he thought. Ronnie's knees buckled, but he didn't go down. He just stood there looking dazed, with his arms dangling, and then Ike hit him in the forehead with the huge, square surface of the knuckles of his right hand. Ronnie's head jerked back like he'd been shot, and he went down to his knees very slowly and then to his face in the dry, brown grass and didn't move.

Ike stood over him for a moment, his great, gray-haired

chest heaving like a big horse, and then he turned and went back across the morning yard to his cottage. Mother Sauls was trying to run across the yard, and Bobby thought at first that she intended to help Ronnie. But then he saw Linda sitting in a heap at the base of her house, holding her belly and crying, and with a presence of mind he hadn't know in a long time, he told Junior to get to the store and call the hospital in Tallahassee to say they were bringing Linda in. Junior took off running.

"What's the doctor's name?" Bobby called to Mother Sauls. He was now standing over Ronnie's crumpled, inert form. "Junior's going to call."

"Peterson," said Mother Sauls. "Dr. Peterson."

"Peterson, Junior," Bobby called. Junior waved his hand that he had understood and disappeared into the store. Bobby kneeled down to examine Ronnie. He was out cold.

"I think she's started," said Mother Sauls. "Is he dead?"

"No," Bobby said. "He ain't dead. Ike didn't hit him *that* hard."

"Did you see his head snap back?" said Mother Sauls.

"I saw it," Bobby said. "But he ain't near dead. He's breathing too hard to be dead."

"I'm getting her to the hospital," said Mother Sauls. "This is awful." She was trying with great difficulty to get Linda to her feet. Linda was sobbing. Mother Sauls's feet were far apart and firmly planted, but even though she was pushing like a stevedore, she could not slide Linda back up the wall she had come down. "Come help me," said Mother Sauls. Together, they got Linda to her feet and walked her between them the fifty yards to the car, which was parked outside the store by the shimmering asphalt road. Junior came bounding out the front door as they got there. "They said to bring her into the emergency room," he said. "Is she going to have the baby?"

"We think so," said Mother Sauls. "I don't know how she can help it with all this shit going on. Come on, honey. We're taking you to the hospital. Hold on." She put Linda in the front seat, then went around and got in on the driver's side. "Are you coming?" she said to Bobby.

"Yes," he said, "if it's all right."

"Get in," said Mother Sauls. She started the engine and called out to Junior through Linda's window. "You stay here," she said. "And stay out of the way if they start in to killing each other again. Just let them do it."

"Yes, ma'am," Junior said.

Bobby watched the pine flatwoods of the St. Joe Paper Company speed by. They were halfway to the hospital in Tallahassee, and Linda's pains had not increased in frequency or intensity. They were still coming about eight minutes apart. "I think we're going to make it," Mother Sauls said. Linda had not spoken. She'd been crying when they got into the car, but now she'd stopped, and neither Bobby nor Mother Sauls had pressed her about the fight.

Bobby watched the woods slide by and thought about Junior's frightened face when they'd left. Poor Junior. They hardly ever let him in on what was really happening— although he still managed to keep his nose in everything. When he was old enough to listen, Mother Sauls had lied and told him his father had been killed in Vietnam, instead of by his own hands. Linda had been five then and knew what had really happened. But after the suicide, when Linda and Junior's mother had abandoned them,

Mother Sauls and Bobby told Linda to go along with the war story for Junior's sake, and she always had, and now Bobby could not remember why.

But it was true, anyway, Bobby thought. Vietnam *had* killed him. Jim had pulled two tours there, in 1966 and '67, and came back sullen and morose and unable to sleep. He'd walked the beach a lot, going out alone in an oyster boat all day, and then, six weeks after his son Junior was born, in 1969, when the rest of them were picnicking with the baby on the beach, he had killed himself in that cottage.

They'd all heard the blast and knew what had happened. It was almost like they had been waiting for it all along and had gone to the beach to give him the time, because nobody moved at the sound. There was a long silence in which they looked at the sand or out at the Gulf, and then Mother Sauls said softly, and as though she were reading it, "He's done it, oh, my God, he's done it." Bobby got to his feet and said, "I'd better go see."

He found Jim's body next to the bed, and the whole top of his head was gone. There was blood and bits of brain and bone stuck to the ceiling. Bobby covered Jim's body with a bloody sheet and then he left the cottage and went into the store to call the sheriff. Then he went back down toward the beach. The others were still gathered in a little knot there on the sand with the Gulf sliding and rolling behind them. Jim's wife, Cathy, was holding Junior. Clear-eyed and expressionless, she watched Bobby coming all the way down the yard from the cottage. It seemed to him as he looked at her, with her eyes the same color as the Gulf, that he was looking through two holes in her face to the water behind. Slowly and with great care, she handed the baby over to Mother Sauls and walked off. She was gone the rest of the afternoon, and in the morning she wrapped Junior in newspaper and left him in a box on the porch and was gone for good.

Bobby reached up over the back of the front seat of the car and stroked Linda's hair. She lifted a hand and placed it on his. "Are you all right?" he asked.

"Fine, Granddad," she said. "I just hope this is it. I'm ready. Do you think Ronnie's all right? I didn't mean to go into this right now."

"He's fine," Bobby said. "He just got the shit kicked out of him. We'll call from the hospital. Junior will let him know how you are."

"Good," Linda said. "I hope he isn't hurt, even if he is bullheaded." She gripped her armrest and grimaced as another pain came and passed.

"Hang on," said Mother Sauls. "We're almost there."

They were into the outskirts of Tallahassee. Linda had another long, bad contraction, and when it was over Bobby said, "What happened back there, anyway?"

"Ronnie saw Ike in the yard," Linda said, when she had caught her breath, "and went busting out the door yelling at him. There wasn't any provocation that I saw. Ike was just walking down to the beach. Ronnie and I had been talking about going into town for some baby clothes, or something, and then he saw Ike and went charging out."

"He's a mess," Bobby said, leaning back in the seat.

"Leave her alone," said Mother Sauls. "She's going to have a baby."

But she didn't have the baby then. The doctor said it was a false labor brought on by all the excitement. Linda should go back home and wait; it might be two weeks yet. The contractions had stopped, but Linda was very upset and exhausted. They let her rest in one of the rooms in the obstetrics unit, and Bobby and Mother Sauls went down to the cafeteria.

Mother Sauls took her cup of coffee and went off to phone Junior, to tell him they'd be back late and to check on Ronnie. Bobby sat at a round table under fluorescent lights in the near-empty, too-cool cafeteria, watching a cluster of young nurses on break. They all looked very tired. He sipped at the coffee. It was hot and very bitter, as if it had been sitting a long time. He watched Mother Sauls come across the floor, carefully winding her way through the tables and chairs, balancing her coffee.

"Ronnie's all right," she said, sitting down. "Junior said he stayed in his cottage all day. He said it sounded like Ike was tearing up *his* place, though. I wonder why?"

"Ike hates to fight," Bobby said. "He's good at it, but he hates it."

"Men are so stupid," she said. "They really are."

Bobby had no reply. He was working on an explanation of the world from an idea he had gotten on the way into town from the coast that morning. He was deciding that everything was motivated and determined by man's pursuit and woman's defense of what lay at the junction of a woman's legs.

"Don't you agree?" prodded Mother Sauls. "Aren't men stupid?"

Bobby sat up and paid attention. He thought from the tone in her voice that she might be making another of her frequent and subtle references to that huge silent thing between them, the woman on the ice route, but she just looked at him and smiled. "Aren't men stupid?" she said again.

"I know I am," Bobby said. "Is that what you want to hear?"

"It helps a little," she said. "But then, I know you've known it a long time. About some things, anyway. We've both known that a long time, haven't we." She finished her coffee, tucked a paper napkin down inside the cup and dropped it in the wastebasket. "Linda's going to be very disappointed she didn't get to have her baby this trip."

Bobby finished his coffee in silence, and Mother Sauls looked around the cafeteria at the nurses and the few visitors—family members with crumpled, sad faces. Then they went upstairs together and got Linda and started back to the Gulf.

Mother Sauls drove again. Linda took the back seat so she could spread out a little more, and Bobby rode by the front window and stared out at the palmettos and pines between Tallahassee and the coast and thought about nothing.

In the morning Bobby was at Ike's again before nine o'clock, to hear his account of the fight. He found Ike in the living room, cleaning up after the destruction of the day before. Some of the furniture was broken, and there was garbage from the kitchen thrown all about the house. Ike was sitting in the middle of the floor, sorting through garbage and pieces of furniture.

"What the hell happened here?" Bobby asked when he came in.

"I tore it up," Ike said. "What the hell do you think happened?"

"I don't know," said Bobby.

"That's right," Ike said. "You don't know, do you."

"But, what happened?" Bobby said.

"I'll fix it, I'll fix it," Ike said. "Can't you see I'm fixing it already?"

"I mean, why'd you do it?" Bobby pulled over one of the chairs that had gone with Ike's séance table and sat in it backward.

"I was pissed," Ike said. "I didn't really want to cool that fucker, you know."

"I know," Bobby said. "I thought you gave him every chance to get out easy. And then you had to cool him."

"That's right," Ike said. "I had to, didn't I?"

"Sure," Bobby said. "You didn't have any choice. You did it too."

Ike got up off the floor and loomed over Bobby like some great dark cloud making up its mind whether to rain or not. He was wearing a black tee shirt with the red wings of Harley-Davidson on the front and his inevitable denim jeans and boots. Bobby was again amazed how Ike could stand the heat in those clothes. "How's Linda?" Ike asked wearily. "I'm getting sick of this place, you know."

"She's all right," Bobby said. "She didn't have the baby. It was a false alarm."

"I know," Ike said. "Junior told me. You want a beer?"

"Too early for me," Bobby said. "What you need is a little fishing."

"Fuck fishing," Ike said. He went to the red Nauga-hyde sofa and sat down. "You have to get all dressed up to sit in this goddamn thing. Otherwise you stick to it. I thought Vietnam was sticky, but this place is worse."

"Were you in Vietnam?" Bobby asked.

"Yes," Ike said. "Too goddamn long. I was a fucking medic, of all things. Put guys back together to go out and get blown up again."

"My son was in Vietnam," Bobby said.

"Everybody was," Ike said gloomily.

"Let's go fishing," Bobby said. "Just you and me. Out on the flats a little. Maybe there's even a few trout left. I'll get us some live shrimp, and we'll take the skiff and put up the Bimini top and stay all day. It'll be good for us. We need to get away."

"I ain't going nowhere in a boat you're driving," Ike said.

"Shit," said Bobby. "I could do this blindfolded. Come on. I won't let you fall out."

Ike turned his head and looked out through the kitchen and porch, down the shimmering white line of cottages to the flat, blue Gulf. He looked a long time, and then Bobby saw the tears come up in his eyes. Bobby looked at the floor. "Come on," he said. "Let's take the boat out and get some trout, Ike."

"I haven't seen that water change one bit since the spring rains," Ike said. "Not one fucking bit. It's like a drawing or something, or a wall. A painted wall. I think it could make you crazy eventually."

"No," Bobby said, looking out at the scene that was more familiar than even his own breathing. "Other things can make you crazy, but not the water. It's what you think the water means that makes you crazy sometimes."

"It doesn't mean anything," Ike said, looking at Bobby again. "Nothing at all. Like a painted wall."

Bobby listened and was suddenly seized with the memory of young girls dancing in a hot, barnlike room with a wide, oak floor. Their long dresses swept out and caught the gauzy sunlight when they twirled, and their arms and legs were like filaments pulled from a warm, soft core. Bobby and one of the boys from the woods had gone to Tallahassee to look around the college. They sneaked into a building with music coming from it and saw the girls dancing across a wooden floor where sunlight coming through the window seemed to roll instead of stick. It was very beautiful but also very sad to remember, and then he thought he knew why Ike had nearly cried looking down the summer at the Gulf. Some things, like the Gulf and the girls twirling across the floor, could be beautiful and sad at the same time. Maybe all truly beautiful things were like that. Maybe Ike knew that too.

SIX

Dink Maynard rattled his battleship gray, 1956 Ford pickup down the length of the yard in the soft light of the muggy, colorless evening. He rolled to a stop next to the porch where Bobby, Mother Sauls, and Junior had just sat down to a supper of fried fish and corn bread. Dink put one elbow out the window of the truck and his face over the top of that and showed them his wide, toothless, country grin.

"Goddamn," said Mother Sauls. "It's Dink Maynard. Look there, Bobby. Look who it is. We heard you were dead, Dink."

"Naw," Dink drawled. "That was just a rumor. I had pneumony pretty bad back last winter, but I didn't die, I don't think." He scratched his cheek and opened the door of the truck, which protested with a grating, metallic shriek, and then he slowly unfolded from the seat and stood in the grass looking at them. He was somewhere around Bobby's age, but much bigger, with great, wide hands and feet and very long arms that now hung loosely almost to his knees, and he hadn't had a tooth in his mouth since his mid-thirties. He left the truck and moved with some difficulty to the porch and up the steps. Junior got up and held the screen door open for him. Dink stepped inside and stood looking down at Junior.

"Who the hell are you?" he said roughly.

"That's Junior," Mother Sauls said. "Jim's boy. Ain't he big, Dink?"

"Son of a bitch," Dink Maynard said, roughing up Junior's hair. "I ain't seen you in ten years, boy."

"You ain't been around in ten years," Bobby said.

"You neither," said Dink. He crossed the porch and stood over Bobby and Mother at the card table they had set up for supper. He put one big hand on Bobby's shoulder and smiled, showing his pink-and-black mottled gums.

"Won't you have something to eat, Dink?" said Mother Sauls. "There's plenty."

"I believe I'll have a piece of corn bread," Dink said. "But that's all, thank you." He looked around for another chair, found one by the screen, and dragged it over to the table. Junior sat looking at Maynard work on the corn bread.

"Where you been?" Bobby said.

"Same," Dink answered. "In the woods."

"And Susie?"

"She's dead. Five, six years ago," Dink said, licking the butter from his fingers. "Heart attack. I was out hunting and when I came back she was sitting on the porch. I thought she was sleeping. I didn't know she was dead until it was suppertime and she didn't go into the kitchen.

They had to cut her tendons to straighten her arms and legs again."

"I'm sorry, Dink," said Mother Sauls.

"It was her time," Dink said.

Bobby glanced up from the table out to the level, blue-gray serenity of the Gulf. He could smell the oyster shells piled under the house and see a floating raft of seaweed with a gull riding on it bobbing and bounding on the gentle swell a few yards offshore. It felt good to see Dink Maynard again after so long. From the time they were boys, Bobby had always been happy when Dink was around. Then he remembered the fight that had been the cause of their ten-year separation. He looked down across the table, and Dink was smiling at him.

"You and me's going out on the town," Dink said.

"There ain't no town," Bobby said.

"Just the same, we're going. Just like the old days. Come on. I got the truck gassed up and everything. We're going drinking."

"Oh, my God," said Mother Sauls. "I thought we'd gotten through all that with you two."

"No, ma'am," said Dink. "Just a little pause there. We're on the road again."

"Couple of old fools," she said.

Dink Maynard stood and put his hands on his hips. "Come on," he said to Bobby. "Do I have to drag you out of here?"

Bobby looked up at Dink a long time, and then he looked at Mother Sauls, who shrugged and looked down at her food. "Do what you want," she said.

"Let me get some smokes," Bobby said. He stood and wiped his hands and threw his napkin at Junior. "Too

bad you can't go," he said. "It'd be a real education."
Junior smirked and Bobby went into the bedroom and got
two packs of cigarettes from his night table. Dink Maynard was already sitting in the truck with the motor running when he got back out to the porch. Mother Sauls
did not look up, and Bobby said nothing as he went
through the screen door and out into the yard.

"Good-bye, Granddad," Junior called. Bobby waved and
got into the truck. Dink immediately handed him a half-
full pint of whiskey and, without looking, started backing
the old truck up the yard. Bobby took a long pull of the
whiskey and watched the Gulf receding in the windshield. Dink hit the blacktop with his back tires, spun the
truck out onto the road, and slammed it into low gear.
They oozed out into the evening, with Dink slapping the
big hollow door of the truck and yelping like a dog with
a treed raccoon.

They had been born within a few weeks of each other
on adjacent farms, in the woods behind the marshes and
estuaries of the coast. They had been best friends all their
lives until the incident ten years before, when Bobby had
accused Dink of underhandedly trying to buy a piece of
land on the river that Bobby'd set his mind on. Dink said
it was every man for himself, and there had been a lot
of name-calling. As it turned out, neither of them got
the land, but they'd stopped speaking and hadn't seen
each other in ten years, until Dink drove up into the
yard.

Bobby drank from the whiskey bottle and passed it back
to Dink. "Where the hell are we going?" he said.

"You want to go into town? We could roll into a bar
somewhere if you want."

"No," Bobby said. "There ain't nothing there. Let's just go back in the woods and drink. How about old Kitchen's place? It's empty, and it's got a great porch, remember?"

"Can't," Dink said. "Some hippies is living there. Not as many as there used to be, but they're still out there."

"Well, I don't give a shit, then," Bobby said. "Wherever." He reached in his pocket for a Camel. It was the time between night and day in which everything seemed to stand still. The whiskey was feeling good in his head, and his knees, where the pain had been all day, were growing numb.

"Goddammit, let's go on back to Crowder's Sink, then," Dink said loudly, slapping the steering wheel. "We can throw shit in the water and cuss loud as we want. And I got two more bottles just like that one." He looked over at Bobby and showed his gums.

"Fine," Bobby said, "but I ain't been there in twenty-five, thirty years. I'm not sure I know the way."

Dink handed back the bottle and spit out the window. "You don't have to know," he said. "I'm driving, and I go there all the time to sneak up on the young folks fucking."

"You do?"

"Yep."

"Will there be any there tonight?"

"What day is it?"

"I don't know. Thursday, I think."

"Probably not," Dink said. "They're mostly out there on the weekends, but there may be a stray or two. We'll check it out."

"I hope so," Bobby said. "I haven't seen a good fuck in a long time. Not since we caught my brother, Jack, and old Blountstown Sally out at Granddaddy's that night. Remember?"

"I remember," Dink said. "She nearly shit. We had a black snake, and we threw it in on them."

"I'd forgotten that," Bobby said. "I just remember watching them."

They rode on down the coast road for another fifteen minutes, and then Dink turned onto a dirt road that went off darkly into the trees. In the last, faded light of the day, Bobby was sure it wasn't the right road. He remembered there being two big oaks just after you came in off the coast road, but they weren't there. The road forked, and between them was a single giant pine, but no oaks. The woods grew thick and tangled close up to the road, with its twin white sandy ruts shining brightly in the lights of the truck. Dink stopped at the fork and took the bottle from Bobby.

"This isn't right," Bobby said. "I thought you said you came here a lot."

"I come in the back way, asshole. I never come this way."

"Well this isn't it," Bobby said. "I know that."

"It really doesn't matter," Dink said calmly. "All the roads back here lead to the sink. They crisscross a lot, but they all come out the same. I'm just trying to find the best one."

"Bullshit," Bobby said, and he took back the bottle. It was nearly empty.

Dink put the truck in gear again and started down the road to the left. It was almost completely dark, but with the headlights they could see straight ahead well enough. It looked as if no one had been down the road in a long time. There were branches and vines coming across nearly all along the way. They bumped along without speaking for a few minutes, and then Bobby saw someone ahead walking in the road.

"Whoa," he said. "What the hell is that?"

Dink revved the motor, but the person in the road did not turn around. He was walking with his head down under a little brown felt hat, and he was wearing coveralls. Dink honked the horn when they were only a few feet from the man. He jumped to the side, whipping his hat off, and turned to face them. Bobby got a good look at him. It was an old black man with close-cropped white hair, and he was carrying a paper bag with a bottle in it. He stood in the palmettos at the side of the sandy road and glared at the truck.

"It's old Cleveland," Dink said. "He lives out here somewhere. He'll know where the sink is." He cut off the engine and leaned over Bobby to yell out that window.

"That ain't Cleveland," Bobby said. "Cleveland used to cut wood for Granddaddy—Cleveland ain't that old."

Dink laughed hard. "Hey, Cleveland," he yelled. "What the hell are you doing? You lost?"

Cleveland put his hat back on his head and stepped closer to the window. He looked at Bobby and then peered in to see who was doing the talking.

"Oh, it's you, Mr. Dink. Shit no, man. I been down to the store for my wine, and I'm heading back home now. Are *you* lost?"

"Hey, Cleveland," Bobby said. "It's Bobby. Remember me?"

Cleveland stuck his head all the way in the window so

that Bobby had to back up a little. He examined Bobby's face. "I do now," he finally said. "You've gotten old as shit, Bobby."

"Well, goddammit, you have too," Bobby said. "I didn't know you lived out here."

"Yep. Have for thirty-five years."

"I don't live far from here," Bobby said. "Over at the cottages there on the beach."

"I know where you stay," Cleveland said. "I stop in the store sometimes for my supplies." He held up the bottle in the bag so Bobby could see it. "I don't never see you, though."

"I'm mostly parked down by the water," Bobby said.

Cleveland nodded and patted Bobby on the shoulder, then stepped back away from the truck again. His face was warm and soft, and he was smiling without teeth, the way Dink did. Bobby remembered they had often fished together on many occasions at the pond on Bobby's grandfather's farm before the farm and all the woods around it were burned. After that he never saw Cleveland again.

"Look here, Cleveland," Dink said. "We're looking for Crowder's Sink. We headed the right way?"

"You are if you don't mind weaving around a bit," Cleveland answered.

"Well, get in, dammit," Dink said. "And show us where it is. We got to get there in time to see the fucking. Hop in."

Cleveland nodded and started climbing into the bed of the truck. Bobby got one of the fresh bottles from under Dink's fishing hat on the seat. "I'm going back there too," he said. "Me and Cleveland's gonna get drunk while you drive."

"Shit," Dink said. He waited until Bobby and Cleveland were seated in the bed with their backs against the cab and their legs stretched out toward the missing tailgate, and then he ground the gears and lurched on down the sandy road, driving with his head stuck out the window to pick up the directions sporadically thrown out into the night by Cleveland.

"Bear on off to the right, Dink," Cleveland said. "This here goes right by my house. You go straight and you run into nothing but trees."

"We want to get to Crowder's Sink," Dink shouted.

"What you think I'm doing?" Cleveland yelled back. He settled back against the cab and took the bottle offered by Bobby. "Old Dink, he's a natural, hard-driving man, ain't he, Mr. Bobby?"

"I reckon," Bobby said.

"Yonder's where I stay," Cleveland said. "Slow down, Mr. Dink."

Dink stopped the truck abruptly and stuck his head out the window. "You ain't going home, are you? Goddamn, Cleveland, that's no way to act. We got bottles of good whiskey here."

Cleveland slowly climbed out of the back of the truck. Several small children ran up from Cleveland's house and stood bashfully watching Bobby and Dink. Dink was making funny faces at them, but they weren't smiling. A young woman sat on the porch, rocking a baby in her arms. Bobby could barely make them out in the low, yellow light coming from a lantern on a table in the house.

"Ya'll go on. I got mine here," Cleveland said, holding up his paper bag. "You just keep going and you'll run right into Crowder's. I'm too old to be gallivantin'."

"Bullshit," Dink said. "All right. We'll catch you next

time, Cleveland." He revved up the motor and fought to find the right gear.

"So long, Cleveland," Bobby said. "It was good to see you again. Maybe I'll see you around the store."

"Maybe," Cleveland said. Dink jerked the truck, and Bobby, still in the back and still holding the bottle of liquor, fell forward. He straightened himself and worked his way back to the cab and watched Cleveland and the kids in the stream of yellow light from the house amid the thickness of palmettos and vines. And then they disappeared in the murky brown shadows along the road. He was left looking at the two ruts of white sand illuminated to a soft pink by the truck's single red taillight. And he was feeling wonderfully drunk.

Crowder's Sink was a spring-fed hole created by the collapse of the earth over a limestone cavern. A beautiful, clear green on sunny days, it was about fifty yards across at its widest point, and estimates of its depth ran from sixty feet to bottomless. Kids who claimed to have gone down in the water with scuba gear said the bottom was layered with beer cans and that there was an intact 1947 Chevrolet on a ledge at eighty feet. Bobby liked the part about the car, and he believed it, sometimes imagining its motor was still running down there in the green water that grew colder with every foot.

Dink circled the sinkhole on the road around its perimeter. There were no other cars. In the clear space above the sink Bobby could see the thick, knotted rope used for a swing. It was still hanging from the massive oak limb that jutted out over the water, which was a flat, slick surface, broken only by the random activity of insects and the sudden movement of the small fish that fed on them. Dink backed the truck up to one of the big rocks that marked the edge of that side of the sink. He got out, came around, and climbed into the pickup bed, next to Bobby. They had a clear view of the entire sink and the road coming in from the other side. Dink lit a cigarette and opened another bottle. "One for each," he said. "If you can't finish yours, give it back."

"I'll finish it," Bobby said. It felt like it had only been a few days instead of ten years since he last went drinking with Dink. It had been a weekly thing with them, interrupted only by Bobby's stint with the CCC and Dink's service in the Pacific during World War II. When Dink came back, they'd tied on a drunk that lasted more than three days, and Bobby woke up in a room in Jacksonville, not knowing how he got there or where Dink had gone. Bobby'd hitchhiked back to the Gulf, and a few days later Dink showed up at the cottages they had recently acquired. But he wouldn't give in to Bobby's persistent questioning. Bobby still didn't know what had happened, and if there were women involved, he felt better not knowing.

Dink finished his cigarette and tried to flick it into the water, but it landed on the big rock in front of them, bounced, and rolled off. "So, what you been doing, Sauls?" he said.

"Nothing. Taking it easy."

"You ever go out in the boats anymore?"

"No, I gave it up for good. I go out to fish some, but that's about it. What about you?"

"I make cypress clocks and sell them," Dink said. "And cypress tables and such. Can't make enough of them. I think they're ugly as shit, but folks like them. I do that and drink and smoke as much as I can."

"Me too," Bobby said. He lit a Camel and blew the

smoke at his feet. Headlights appeared on the road across
the sink from them, then cut off. Bobby saw a late-model
sedan quietly roll up to the bank.

"This could be it," Dink whispered. "Do you think they
saw us?"

"I don't know," Bobby answered. "I don't think so. We
blend in pretty well here under the trees."

"We'll give them a little time, and then we'll sneak up
on them, all right?"

"Sure." Bobby looked closely at Dink's face. Dink was
nearly cross-eyed, and his lips were peeled back in an apparently permanent smile over his toothless gums.

"Put out your smoke," Dink said slyly. "And don't light
any for a while."

"Right," Bobby said.

Ten minutes passed. They sat drinking from their bottles and watching the motionless car. Then Dink put his
finger to his lips, put his bottle down, and started over
the side of the truck. He crouched next to the wheel.
Bobby looked over, and Dink motioned him to come down
too.

"We may have to crawl," Dink whispered when Bobby
was on the ground next to him.

"That shouldn't be too hard," Bobby said.

"Follow me," Dink said. He led the way in a semi-
crouch. Bobby followed him back through the woods, away
from the sink. Dink found a path of sorts that seemed to
circle the hole. He started down that with Bobby right
behind. Suddenly, Dink fell off the path in a loud crashing of sticks, and Bobby hung back a little until Dink
went down on all fours near the parked car. They were
coming up behind it, having gone around the sink, and

Dink went from his knees to his belly and looked back to be sure Bobby was doing the same. He motioned to Bobby to go around on the right side of the car and that he was going to take the left. Bobby wasn't sure what he was supposed to do once he got there, but it didn't matter anymore. He was having fun.

Dink slithered on his belly like a huge, badly injured snake. But Bobby got back into his crouch and inched toward the car with his feet under him so he could get away quickly if he had to. The window on his side was down, but he couldn't see anyone inside. He stepped very carefully so he wouldn't make any noise looking over, he saw Dink stand and crane his neck so he could see inside the car. Bobby moved right up to the back window and peered down inside. All he saw at first was someone's naked bottom, and then he saw the girl's face. And she saw his in the same instant. She screamed and threw the boy off with a mighty kick of her legs, which sent him banging his head against the top of the car. And she kept screaming and trying to find something to cover herself with, but there was nothing there. Bobby got a good look at her naked, screaming on the back seat, and then he beat it for the woods while the boy was trying to make a little sense of what was going on. Bobby heard Dink laughing above the girl's screaming all the way back around the sink to the truck, and then they heard the car start and go crashing off.

Bobby got to the truck first. He was drinking from a near-empty bottle when Dink came dragging up, covered with dirt and leaves and scratches from the vines.

"Hey," he said breathlessly. "She wasn't bad, was she, Bobby?"

"I bet she's still trying to get dressed." Bobby laughed. "Did you see that little fucker bounce off the roof?"

"We did them a favor," Dink said. "That's something they can remember all their lives. 'The great goddamn scary fuck at Crowder Sink.' I love it. We've got to do this more often."

"I've missed you, old Dink," Bobby said. "You're one hell of a bad influence."

"Sure," Dink said.

They climbed back into the truck bed and leaned up against the cab and looked at the still water of the sink while they drank and smoked. Then Dink dozed off, and Bobby stood on wobbly knees and took a leak over the side while the pines turned in a circle overhead. There was only the sliver of a moon, and it was caught in the top of the great oak whose massive, horizontal limb went out unbelievably far over the sink. But there were thousands of stars, and a good many of them were falling in the long yellow stream Bobby let over the side of the truck. And a good many more were floating in the black, motionless water of Crowder's Sink.

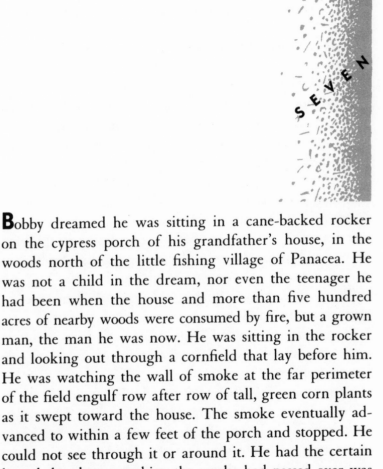

SEVEN

Bobby dreamed he was sitting in a cane-backed rocker on the cypress porch of his grandfather's house, in the woods north of the little fishing village of Panacea. He was not a child in the dream, nor even the teenager he had been when the house and more than five hundred acres of nearby woods were consumed by fire, but a grown man, the man he was now. He was sitting in the rocker and looking out through a cornfield that lay before him. He was watching the wall of smoke at the far perimeter of the field engulf row after row of tall, green corn plants as it swept toward the house. The smoke eventually advanced to within a few feet of the porch and stopped. He could not see through it or around it. He had the certain knowledge that everything the smoke had passed over was gone—not just burned, but gone. All that was left was Bobby, the porch, and the house behind him, but he was not afraid.

The smoke hovered and rolled before the insignificant

cypress slats of the porch steps, and then a figure that was definitely a man, but without a face, stepped fully formed out of the smoke and ascended the porch. The figure motioned Bobby to follow and then opened the screen door and went into the house. Bobby got out of his rocker and followed. Inside, on the left as he came in, there was a door that had never been there before. The smoke figure motioned Bobby to open the door and enter. Bobby did so and found himself in a primitive dumbwaiter, which started going up as soon as he stepped in. He experienced a feeling of great joy, rising in that dumbwaiter, but he woke up before it got where it was going.

Linda was standing over him. Bobby could hear a mockingbird's incessant catalog of calls nearby; it was nearly as beautiful as his dream. He stared for a moment at Linda's round, luminous face before recognizing it, thinking he was still in the dream and that the mockingbird was a part of it too.

"I was dreaming," Bobby said. He rolled his eyes to clear away the cobwebs.

"I'm sorry, Granddad," Linda said. "I didn't want to wake you like this, but I need to talk to you. Have you been asleep long?"

"I don't know," Bobby answered. "What time is it?"

"After four. It's clouding up. It looks like it might finally rain." Linda was dragging one of the other porch chairs next to Bobby's so that she could look out at the Gulf too. Neither of them spoke. Bobby closed his eyes to listen to the mockingbird. He knew what the dream had been about, and he believed if he had risen to whatever the top of the dumbwaiter was, he would have been dead, but he was angry that things still came to him in such a

Sunday school manner when he was sure he didn't believe that way anymore. He remembered Linda's bad time at the hospital and sat up straight in the chair.

"Are you all right?" he asked.

"I really want to have this baby," Linda said with some hesitation. "But I'm worried. What if it's born without the finger, Granddad?"

"I told Ronnie that might happen," Bobby said. "He said it was impossible."

"It's not," Linda said wearily. "It's not impossible at all."

"I know," Bobby continued. "It could happen. There might be some fluke, or something. It's bound to happen sometime in this crazy family. We can't all be born with extra fingers." He looked for the first time at the thick buildup of clouds out over the Gulf. If it was going to rain, he would smell it. He heard Linda sigh, but she said nothing for a long time.

"He won't drown it," Bobby finally said, looking at her. "He wants it too much. You'll see."

"I'm trying to tell you this baby could very easily be born without the stupid finger," Linda said. "Don't you understand?"

"Yes!" Bobby said angrily. "I'm agreeing with you, dammit."

Linda tried to stand, but her weight was too much to shift that fast and she sank back into the chair in a grand, floundering gesture of defeat. "Does a house have to fall on you, Bobby? I'm saying the baby might not be Ronnie's. That's how come it might not have the finger."

"Oh," Bobby said. He turned his face away from her and absently watched the roughening water. There was a storm somewhere, he reasoned, but it wasn't coming here, and then he realized he had actually given up hope that it might ever rain on the cottages again. He had given up on the rain but not on Ike's prediction. There had to be more than this.

"There," Linda said with another huge sigh. "I've told you."

"Yes," Bobby said, "you've told me. Who else have you told?"

"No one. I was afraid Ronnie would find out. There was nobody to tell, anyway. I just couldn't keep it in anymore. It was making me crazy. I couldn't tell Grandmother. She would be so stern, and I would feel worse."

"He suspects," Bobby said.

"I know."

"You better make sure he doesn't find out. He'll kill you both."

"But it's not going to have the finger," Linda said through the tears that had started down her face without his knowing it. "He'll know then."

"Maybe not," Bobby said. "I've planted the seed in him." Bobby looked out onto the Gulf again. The clouds were beginning to dissipate. "Who was it?" he said.

"It was when the bikers were here," Linda said. "It happened one night then, just one time."

"Was it Ike?"

"I won't tell you. I can't."

"Maybe it really is Ronnie's," Bobby said. "You don't really know for sure, do you."

"No."

"Then don't worry. We'll cross that bridge when we get to it. I'll take care of Ronnie."

Linda reached over and took one of Bobby's hands in both of hers. They were the softest hands Bobby had felt in many years.

"Do you hate me?" Linda asked him.

"No," Bobby said. "It really doesn't matter. It was just something that happened. You just have to be sure Ronnie never knows for certain—if you want to stay with him—and because you are going to carry the memory of it around, it should always be a happy memory. It will seem like a dream after a while, anyway. No, I don't hate you at all. I'm happy for you and happy you told me."

Linda squeezed Bobby's hand in hers. "You're a dear old Granddad," she said.

"Yes, I am," said Bobby. "Most of the time."

For the next few days, Linda's confession, instead of being troublesome, lifted Bobby's spirits as he sat and watched the water. He lounged on the porch smoking one Camel after another in the syrupy heat, occasionally downing a cold can of beer. He was happy with their little conspiracy, happy that someone he loved was guilty of the same thing as he. Several times he wanted to tell her about the woman on the ice route so that she might feel lighter too, but he knew he could not. Bobby had hoped it had been Ike, and now he knew that it had been. That was the real reason he'd stayed on at the cottages. Ronnie knew too, but there was nothing he could do but wait.

Ronnie waited impatiently, meanly, and from the porch Bobby watched the changes in him. In the evenings Ronnie stalked the beach alone, smoking and throwing shells into the water but speaking to no one. And when he came for Junior in the mornings to go out in the boats and Bobby was there, awake with his cigarettes and coffee, Ronnie was at once furtive and brooding. He would pace the porch until Junior came out, then be quick and aggressive with the boy as he hustled him out into the early morning dark, always without words. Several times following his talk with Linda, Bobby thought he heard Ronnie's angry voice from their cottage, then held his breath until he heard the inevitable slap of their screen door that meant Ronnie was out alone in the dark and Linda was safe.

Linda did not come round again, and Bobby knew she was trusting him to square things with Ronnie about the baby. But he did not talk to Ronnie about it. There was no way to reach him, so Bobby put off confronting him until the baby came, with or without the finger. Knowing how violent Ronnie had become and what he was capable of, Bobby was impressed with his own ability to remain calm. He reveled in the quiet, colorful intensity of Linda's, and his own, ageless dilemma.

And then, quite abruptly, Ronnie reversed himself again and became the social, affable man he had been when he first moved in with Linda at the cottages. The change became apparent on a Sunday afternoon, when, through some power only she possessed, Mother Sauls convinced everyone, including Ike and Mr. Wilkes, to dine together at a long, makeshift plywood table on their porch. Linda and Ronnie arrived arm in arm after everyone else was already there, and Ronnie immediately went over to Ike, who was standing large and gloomy, beer in hand, at the far end of the porch, and offered his hand.

"No hard feelings," Ronnie said. "I was out of line; I'm sorry."

"No hard feelings," Ike said, and he actually smiled.

"It's going to be all right," Linda whispered in Bobby's ear, and he wondered if maybe she'd told Ronnie the whole story and they had worked it out between them.

"Goddamn," Bobby said to himself.

"There," said Mother Sauls. "That's the way a family is supposed to behave. Everyone sit down. I'll get the food."

It was a good dinner, a long overdue dinner, as Mother Sauls called it, of fresh broiled fish, broccoli with cheese sauce, and a good white jug wine, followed by hot peach pie and ice cream. Ronnie was cheerful throughout and drew Wilkes into a lengthy explanation of pool construction, which continued while Ike helped Mother Sauls clear the dishes, dismantle the plywood table, and bring out more beer.

"That's what we need here," Ronnie said. "If we had a pool, this place would be full right now."

"I don't like it full," Bobby said. "Too many people running around. Too many kids. Besides, somebody'd probably drown. Anyway, what do you care? You're never here."

"It'd be great," Ronnie went on. "Junior could be the lifeguard. We'd build him a little tower and get him a whistle and one of those safari hats. It'd be great, wouldn't it, Wilkes?"

"There's plenty of room for one in the middle there," Wilkes said.

"We'd be just like one of them beach motels then," said Ronnie. "Just like Panama City."

"Maybe we'll do it someday," Bobby said.

Ike reappeared on the porch lugging an ice chest full of beer. They all had one, even Junior and Linda, and they talked about pools and fishing. And Bobby went on about the way the coast had been in the thirties and forties and how the fish were nearly all gone now. And then Wilkes thanked them and excused himself, and Ike had one more beer and left too.

"I've got to get the parlor ready," he said. "That old chick is coming tomorrow morning again to talk to her departed husband."

"Good luck," said Bobby.

"She loves me," Ike said. Ronnie stood up and shook Ike's hand again, and Ike went out into the evening heat.

Junior left to go fishing, and Mother Sauls and Linda went off to take naps somewhere in the house, leaving Bobby and Ronnie alone on the porch with the cooler of beer. At first Bobby was very uncomfortable; he hated being alone with Ronnie, not really believing in his transformation. But he was also puzzled by it, and he wanted to know if Linda had told him everything. Ronnie had obviously stayed behind on purpose—ordinarily, he would have bolted from the house immediately after dinner. Pulling two beers from the ice and handing one to Bobby, he situated his chair so he was facing the Gulf. It was turquoise close in and a flat blue-gray, like a highway in the heat, out near the horizon. Bobby wondered if anybody ever sat with his back to the Gulf. Nobody ever had on his porch.

"Linda and I had a long talk," Ronnie said. "All I want is for everything to be all right with this kid. I've been acting crazy; I'm sorry."

"You were worried," Bobby said.

"I'm not anymore. We had a good talk about it, and it's OK now."

Bobby lifted his aching knees and placed his feet on the milk crate at the foot of his chair. He searched carefully for the right words. "What did she tell you?" he asked.

"She made me see how crazy I've been," Ronnie said. "I know now she could never have done the thing I thought. It's just not in her. I should have known that. I know now she really loves me."

"Of course she does," Bobby said. "This has been hard on her."

"I know. I'll make it up to her. We're thinking of moving to Tallahassee when the baby's born. I can't stay in oystering forever."

"It's a good life," Bobby said. He was watching Junior working his way up the beach toward the cottages with his surf rod. Junior was pulling a long line tied to his waist; it stretched into the water. Bobby could see the flashing bodies of several whiting as they turned in the shallows at the end of the line.

"It's a good life," he said.

"Not for a family man," Ronnie said. "Maybe it used to be, but it's not anymore. You know that. It's too hard to keep up. I want them to have more than that. Tallahassee's a pretty big place now. Maybe I'll find something better up there."

"You won't be able to stay away from the water."

"I can try. That's not all there is, you know."

Bobby looked at the Gulf and remembered when he had lived away from it, when he worked with the CCC, and he was gone from the smell of the water and the oyster shells. He remembered the closed-in feeling of the unfamiliar woods and the ache and how much he had missed Mother Sauls and their son. And then he remembered the woman on the ice route and the way the water had looked from her bedroom window and the waving grasses at the mouth of the river there and the smell of the coffee she made.

"You'll be back," he said. "You won't be able to stay away. Everybody comes back."

It was nearly dark when Ronnie and Linda left. Bobby had another cigarette, then left the porch and wandered up through the yard between the cottages. There was a little wind coming off the Gulf, a homeward wind. Bobby remembered it from his days on the water before all the boats had motors; they used to hoist a sail to get back to shore. Like delicate, cool fingers, the breeze slid over the back of his neck as he walked. Bobby meandered up the yard to the road in front of the store and stood out on the pavement, looking first one way and then the other at the empty, black stretch that, before being paved, had once been thick with coquina. Coquina made a good road, Bobby thought. He turned and looked for a time at the huge, palm-shaped sign in front of Ike's cottage, and then he started back down the yard toward the water.

He stopped near Wilkes's cottage and looked at the light in the window for a minute. Then he went up to the screen door and knocked. Wilkes came and stood barefoot in the doorway. Bobby could see the box of bones on the coffee table in the living room behind him.

"How's it going?" Bobby said.

"Fine," said Wilkes. "Out for a little night air?"

"Yes. Listen, I want to talk to you. I know what you're doing in there, and it's fine, but it's pretty damn strange too."

"How do you know?" Wilkes said.

"Junior looked through the window. That's all. I know he shouldn't have, and I gave him hell for it, but you know how kids are. He said you were doing something with bones in there. I'm just curious, is all."

Wilkes looked at him for a long moment in which Bobby heard the cicadas as plainly as if they were lodged in his own ears with the solid curtain of heat behind them. And then Wilkes smiled. "Come in," he said. "I'll show you."

He led the way into the living room and sat on the sofa with the box in front of him. "Please sit down," he said. "I'm sorry. You have a right to know, of course. I didn't mean to be sinister about it. I just wanted to be alone."

"I don't mean to be nosy," Bobby said.

"It's all right. There really isn't any secret. As you can see, I'm assembling a skeleton." He held up the part he had finished. The spine was complete, and he was working on the ribs. "It's very slow, close work."

"I imagine it is," said Bobby. "Why are you doing it?"

Wilkes put the skeleton back in the box and leaned back on the sofa. "This was my son," he said.

Bobby felt a buzzing in his temples that was not the crickets or the cicadas. He was suddenly fearful of Wilkes the way he had been of Ronnie, but he did not know what to be afraid of in Wilkes. He broke from Wilkes's gaze and looked at the floor. "Did you kill him?" he said.

Wilkes uttered a little half-formed, choking laugh. "No," he said. "He died, but nobody killed him."

"I had a son once," Bobby said, still looking at the floor.

"But he killed himself right over there in one of the other cottages. He was a lot bigger than this one, though."

"I'm sorry," Wilkes said. "Yes, this one was very small. Very, very small."

Bobby kept looking at the pine floor. There was a lot more he wanted to ask Wilkes: about the baby's death, and its life, and his seemingly unreal detachment. But he felt he had pried too much already, and the bones being Wilkes's son made him extremely uncomfortable. A further explanation would have to wait. Bobby struggled to his feet and stood in a cone of thick yellow light that poured from the bare bulb in the ceiling. "I'm going now," he said, and then, as an afterthought to ease his embarrassment: "I'll get Mother to send that fan over tomorrow. You must get pretty warm in here."

"That will be fine," Wilkes said. "If it's no bother."

"You'll get it tomorrow," Bobby said. "I'm sorry."

Wilkes walked him to the door, and Bobby went out into the night, into the warm, starlit, Gulf-breeze night that was thick with the confusing memory of babies and lovers—living, dead, and unborn—feeling, perhaps for the first time in his life, as old as he really was.

Psychic Ike found Bobby sitting on the dark porch with his morning coffee and cigarettes even before Ronnie had come to get Junior. It was just before dawn. Bobby was watching lightning flashes out over the Gulf. He imagined he was witnessing a distant battle, with the flashes being big guns firing, and was feeling the old disappointment for having never seen a real battle. He remembered the letters Jim had written from Vietnam, early on, before the letters stopped coming. Jim had described the battle sights and sounds in such wonderful, vivid detail—before it all became first too ugly and then too common. Bobby promised himself to dig out those letters later and read them all again; Mother Sauls would know where they were. He was sorry he had never been in even a little battle, and he was sorry Jim had been in so many big ones.

Ike came onto the porch, grinning. He had trimmed his beard and combed his hair and looked five years younger. He came out of the dark like a surfacing porpoise, smiling the way porpoises smile when they pop up next to a boat. "Hey, old man," he said, "got a minute?"

Bobby was momentarily startled by Ike's appearance. When he had heard the steps groan and the screen door open, he was prepared to see Ronnie, but instead there was this new Ike, spruced up like a Methodist preacher. Bobby only partly stifled a laugh. "Holy shit," he said. "You going to a funeral?"

"Nothing that good," Ike said. "But *I'm* dead if you don't help me with this chick that's coming over this morning to talk to her dear departed."

"I thought you had it covered, you big ape. You said she loved you."

Ike pulled up one of the chairs and sat down heavily. "I'm kind of worried," he said. "I've got to convince her I'm making contact, to keep her coming back. She's got more money than she knows what to do with." He leaned out over toward Bobby with his hands clasped in front of him. "This is it for me, man. I don't have much else to go on. I might need a little help on this one."

"You sound like a desperate man," Bobby said. "What do you want me to do?"

"You can be his voice," Ike said, slapping his knees with open palms. "I really had her going last time, and she did a lot of talking to him, but he hasn't been too hot on answering yet."

"No way," Bobby said, lighting another cigarette. He took a drag and tried to blow the smoke out through the screen but didn't make it. "That's fraud."

"So, since when has that bothered you, old man? You're fraudulent as they come. Don't give me that shit."

Bobby thought Ike was referring to the dead flying fish in the cottage and that he was making fun of him. "I didn't make any of it up," he said. "It really happened. I saw them."

"What are you babbling about? I'm talking about you and Linda. You know that baby ain't Ronnie's, and you're playing it just like everybody else."

"I thought you meant something else," Bobby said, too weary of the whole thing with Linda to get into it with Ike again. "I thought you meant the flying fish."

"Fuck flying fish," Ike said. "I'm trying to hang on here, man."

"Linda and Ronnie have worked everything out," Bobby said to end it. "So I don't know what you're talking about. You ought to stay away from it. Nothing's going to change, even if the baby's born with an extra finger on its ear." He mashed out the cigarette and looked at Ike.

"Just don't sit there pretending you don't know what's happened," Ike said. "That's all I'm saying. Now, listen, are you going to help me, or not? Come on. It might be fun. I came to get Junior too."

"Junior's supposed to go out in the boats," Bobby said. "But I suppose I could tell Ronnie to go ahead without him. What are you going to do?"

"I've got a little plan," Ike said. "But we've got to get going on it. She's coming at ten. Come on, man. Get Junior up, please."

"All right, I will," Bobby said. "But only if you promise to go fishing with me when this is all over. And I get to drive the boat."

"Agreed," said Ike, shaking Bobby's hand. "It's an enormous price, but I'll pay."

Ike headed off at a good clip toward his cottage, and Bobby went inside to wake Junior. Over the Gulf the lightning was gone from the water, and a color like the underside of a dark rose was beginning to appear on the horizon.

Ike did have a plan, and Bobby found out right away what they needed Junior for. He watched as Ike sent the exuberant Junior clambering up a ladder and through a trapdoor in the ceiling of the hallway. Armed with an electric drill and a flashlight, Junior made his way in the crawl space to the center of the room over Ike's séance table.

"I'm glad that's him and not me," Bobby said.

"You'd get lost, and I'm too big," Ike said. "I think of everything." Clutching a hammer, he pushed the table aside and stood on a chair, poised to drive a nail into the ceiling.

"When you see the nail, Junior," Ike called, "that's where I want you to drill."

"Go ahead," came Junior's muffled reply.

Ike put the nail in the dead center of the ceiling. "Do you see it?"

"I've got it," Junior said.

"All right. When I pull it out, you drill on through. Don't lose the spot." He wrenched the nail free, and a moment later they heard the drill. And then the bit splintered through.

"Mother's going to kick our butts," Bobby mused.

"She'll never know," said Ike. "Good, Junior. Come on back, and I'll hand you up the hole saw."

"All right," Junior said.

"When we get this rigged, I'll show you what you have to do," Ike said to Bobby. "This is going to be great. Crude, but great."

Junior drilled a three-inch hole in the ceiling, and then Ike handed him up a small spotlight with a blue filter and a long extension cord. "Put the spot right over the hole and run the cord back out through the trapdoor," he said. "When we get the séance going, you can plug it in down here."

"What's that supposed to do?" Bobby asked.

"She's partial to blue," Ike said. "I told her I was seeing her old man in a blue light. This coming down onto the table will knock her out."

After Junior attached the light and came down from the crawl space, Ike drilled another hole in the tabletop and screwed a small speaker to it from underneath. Then he attached a wire, hid it along a table leg and under a rug, and ran it into the bedroom, where he fixed it to a microphone.

"This is where you'll be," he told Bobby. "I could have used a taped message, but that would have been too general. This way, you can respond to her specific questions."

"What'll I say?" asked Bobby.

"Whatever she wants to hear. You'll know. Just play it by ear. She knows to speak loudly because the spirits are pretty distant, so you won't have any problem hearing her."

"What if I don't sound like her husband?"

"Put a handkerchief over the mike," Ike said. "Anyway, it won't matter. You think she's going to care when she hears somebody answering her?"

"I guess not," Bobby said. Junior came ambling into the bedroom and stood grinning over the wires and paraphernalia. "What about him?" Bobby said, pointing to Junior.

"He can stay with you, as long as he's quiet. Maybe you can do background noise or something, Junior."

"I'll be God," Junior said.

Ike fixed Bobby a pot of coffee, then covered the speaker in the table with his black tablecloth and made sure all the wires were hidden. The three of them sat in the kitchen without speaking while Bobby had his coffee, and then at quarter to ten Ike shooed them into the bedroom. "When I say, 'I can see him,'" Ike told Junior, "you plug the extension cord in right here and leave it."

"Got it," Junior said. "I can see him." He was shifting his weight from one foot to the other in his excitement.

"No noise," Ike said. "This is important. Don't blow it."

"He won't," Bobby said. "He's fraudulent as the rest of us."

Ike went into the living room, and Bobby sat on the bed, looking at Junior. He reached for a cigarette in his shirt pocket, then realized the smell of the smoke might give them away and was proud of himself. He looked at Junior and remembered the tiny bones. "You know those bones Wilkes has in his place?"

"Sure," Junior said. "What about them?"

"That was his son," Bobby said. "Died when he was a baby, and Wilkes is putting him back together."

"How'd he die?" Junior asked.

"I don't know," Bobby said. "He didn't tell me. I think

it wasn't very long ago, though, from the way he talks about it."

"What's he going to do with it, Granddad?"

"I don't know. It's very sad."

Ike stuck his great hairy head in the doorway. "Knock it off," he said. "Her car just pulled up. Remember what you're supposed to do, and keep it quiet. This is it." He closed the door behind him nearly all the way, leaving an opening of two or three inches.

Bobby motioned Junior to join him on the bed, and he put one finger to his lips. Junior nodded and sat down. They heard the screen door whine open and slap shut and some muffled voices, but Bobby could not make out the words. He heard Ike draw the black curtains in the living room and turn on the table fan, and then it was very quiet. Bobby listened to his own breathing and looked at the backs of his brown, mottled hands. Sometimes, in the oyster boats, he used to watch his hands when he pulled up the tongs to *keep* from thinking about the room overlooking the mouth of the St. Marks River and the waving brown grass and the woman there. But now those hands were the entry to that room. Hands that were old, without strength, and covered with thin, brown-paper skin, transported into a room in his memory that was ageless and hermetically sealed. He closed his eyes and scanned its sun-washed walls as if he were standing in the center of that room and turning in a circle.

Junior nudged him in the ribs with an elbow. Bobby opened his eyes, and Junior nodded toward the door. Ike was speaking. Junior eased off the bed and picked up the plug of the extension cord.

"O spirits of the Great Beyond," Ike said. "O great

gathering of souls departed but not forgotten. Hear me. We wish to make contact. Hear me, spirits. There is someone who wishes with all her heart to communicate with the dearly departed."

"John?" said a woman's frail voice, then stronger, "John?"

"Concentrate," Ike said. "We respectfully request contact with the spirit of John Silvy, O realm beyond words. John Silvy, can you hear me?"

Junior looked questioningly at Bobby, the plug in his hand nearly touching the outlet. Bobby shook his head no.

"John Silvy," Ike boomed, "your wife wishes contact. Make yourself known."

"Please, John," came the woman's voice. "It's me. Margaret."

"I'm getting something," Ike said excitedly. "I'm definitely getting something. I see a soft blue light and something behind it. There is a shape, but I can't make out what it is. Is that you, John Silvy? Make yourself known. Communicate with us. Shave away the distance and be clear to us."

"Is it him?" the woman said. "Oh, John."

"I can't tell. Wait a minute. Yes, there is a man. I can see him!"

Bobby waved vigorously at Junior, who immediately plugged in the cord.

"Oh, my God," the woman gasped. "The light, the blue light. It is him. Oh, John."

Bobby reached for the microphone, but it wasn't there. Junior had crawled to the door and was on his hands and knees there, watching, with his back to Bobby. The microphone was nowhere to be found.

"Pssst," Bobby hissed. "Where's the fucking mike?"

Junior whirled around with a look of panic on his face.

"I can see him, but I can't hear him," Ike bellowed.

Junior was pawing around on the floor for the microphone wire. He found it and ran his hand along it to the bed. The microphone was on the bed where Ike had put it, under a pillow. Junior pulled it out and they heard a scratching sound amplified into the living room. Bobby snatched the mike from Junior and put it to his mouth.

"John? Can you hear me," the woman said. "Are you there? Is that really you?"

"It's me," Bobby said, as deeply and spiritually as he could. His voice boomed and resonated all over the house.

"We come in love and friendship," Ike said. "Will you hear us, spirit?"

"I will hear you," said Bobby. "Ask me anything."

"Where are you, John?" the wife asked.

"A beautiful place," Bobby said. "It's very beautiful." He was imagining the room overlooking the mouth of the river, and the waving brown grass.

"Is it far?"

"Very far."

"Tell me about it," the woman implored. "I want to know if you're comfortable. I want to know all about it."

"I'm fine," Bobby said. "My knees hurt every now and then, but I'm all right." Junior was holding back his laughter with both hands. "The place is fine and there are friends and relatives." Bobby continued. "We have a pretty good time, all in all, but being dead's not all it's cracked up to be. We don't get much news from back home, except when somebody dies, and then they're not too talkative, for a while anyway. It's real good to hear from you."

"I've tried contacting you before, John. I knew you were nearby, but I couldn't break through. It's so hard. I've missed you so much."

"Me too," said Bobby. "We had some good times together, didn't we?"

"The best," came the woman's voice. "It's what I think about all day long. It keeps me going."

"That's good," Bobby said. "I think about it a lot too. I remember things without trying, and then I get lost in them and stay a long time. Mostly I remember the same things over and over, like the river and the Gulf out beyond it. But sometimes I think of something new, and that is very good because there is no future to think about. I have a lot of time on my hands, and I remember our good times when I'm looking out at the water."

"Oh, John. Can you see the Gulf from where you are? I was hoping you could, but I didn't know how those things worked where you are."

"I can't see it right now," Bobby said. "But it's mostly what I do."

"Is it the same?"

"It changes every day, like it always has, so in that way it's the same, yes. It doesn't go anywhere, and neither do I." Bobby closed his eyes and imagined the Gulf beyond the dark mouth of the river, where her house had been, to the green flats where you could wade waist-deep for nearly a mile. He wanted to describe it that way aloud, because saying it made the picture solid, made it last longer. But she wanted to know what he saw now. Bobby had forgotten the woman in the other room was one of Ike's customers. He thought he was talking to *her* again. "It is the same Gulf," he said. "But it was more beautiful then. You remember that."

"I'm starting to lose him," Ike said, and Bobby opened his eyes. Junior was watching him, mesmerized. Bobby signaled him to get ready to pull the plug, and Junior's eyes went suddenly alert.

"There he goes," Ike said. "I think that's all we can manage now."

"John," the woman said, "I'll be back. I love you."

"I'll be here," Bobby said softly into the mike, then laid it on the bed and took a deep breath. Junior pulled the plug on the extension cord, and they could hear the woman crying from the living room. Bobby sat looking at his hands.

In a few minutes they heard the screen door open and close again and then Ike opened the bedroom door. He was showing them his great barroom smile. "We did it," he said. "She bought the whole damn thing. You were great, Bobby. But I had to cut you off when you started getting so weird about the water and everything. You do that a lot, man." He stooped to gather the extension cord and started wrapping it between his hand and elbow. "But it worked," he continued. "I think it was good not to give her too much. She'll definitely be back now. You were great."

"I was talking to someone else," Bobby said. "It was the only way I could do it. I hope it was all right."

"You were fine," Ike said. "But you scare the shit out of me sometimes. Come on. Let's have a beer. You too, Junior. I wish you guys could have seen that old chick's face. She was straight out of 'Twilight Zone,' man. I tell you what, I'm getting pretty good at this gig."

"**W**here were you all morning?" Mother Sauls asked. "You didn't show up on the porch until nearly two, and you slept from then on." They were alone in the kitchen, eating a supper of fried pork chops and mashed potatoes. It was nearly dark. With the slow descent of the beige evening in the kitchen, Mother Sauls had not bothered to turn on a light. Now that the light was almost gone from the room, there was a soft-edged feel to everything, and Bobby languished in the comfort of it.

"I was helping Ike," he said. "Me and Junior."

"Junior was with you? He was supposed to be working."

"He was working," Bobby said. "We helped Ike with a very successful séance. He doesn't have to go out in the boats every day."

Mother Sauls did not answer. She sat across the table from him in the sad light and drank her after-dinner coffee. Bobby lit a cigarette. Then, remembering the woman at Ike's, he placed his hand on top of hers, along the outer edge of the table. The skin was soft and cushiony. She quickly withdrew it as she had done each time he'd initiated contact in the past fifty years. Bobby pulled in his hand and took the cigarette from his lips. He had grown so used to her reactions to his touch that he rarely noticed anymore. But this time, again because of the woman they had fooled at Ike's, his wife's instinctive or carefully controlled withdrawal was a sudden and painful reminder of their separation.

"It was a woman who wanted to talk to her dead husband," he said. "At Ike's. It was very nice."

"Did she?"

"Yes." Bobby could barely make out her sagging, waxy features in the vanishing light.

"Did he answer?"

"Yes."

"What did he say?"

"He said he was sorry," Bobby answered.

There was a light in the bedroom of Jim's cottage when Bobby went by it on his way up to the road. He stood in the yard and watched the unchanging yellow glow for a long time, until his fear dissolved. Then he went up onto the porch of the cottage and let himself in through the kitchen.

He could see the light spilling over into the hallway from the bedroom. It was not lamplight, but something clearer, thinner, softer. He passed through the living room and into the short, narrow hallway.

The bedroom, her bedroom, was washed in the light of a morning off the marsh. Bobby could smell the river in the light, and the brown, waving grasses there. The bed had been made in fresh white sheets with small yellow flowers, and there were flowers with purple centers in a wine bottle on the nightstand. Of course, the pale sunlight went halfway up the wall behind the bed, for this was the room where it was always morning. He would not have recognized it any other way. Bobby caressed the room once with his glance and left the cottage, the distant morning light from the bedroom still falling in a thin film onto the black grass of the yard.

He had a cigarette on the porch and then went in to bed. Mother Sauls was already there in her own bed, sprawled in a light cotton gown, but he could tell by her breathing she wasn't asleep. Bobby undressed and lay on his back in the sticky, militant heat, while the crickets and cicadas gradually surfaced in his consciousness. He heard Mother Sauls stir, then get out of bed. She stood next to his bed and dropped her nightgown to the floor, then slowly brought herself next to him. Her body was strangely fragrant and cool against his skin.

"It's time again," she said, using the same words she always used. "Do what you're supposed to do."

NINE

From shore, the squall looked to be some three miles wide, with gracefully tapered, nearly symmetrical right and left sides curving up into a great, dark, towering column of cloud. The top was blown off into the shape of a white, feathery anvil that disappeared into pale blue above it. At the base of the column of cloud and all along the distended width of the gray squall, the curiously stiff filaments of blue rain were curving into the surface of the water. The entire system was moving slowly shoreward from the Gulf. Mother Sauls was the first to notice it that morning, when after breakfast she went out to hang sheets on the line. Bobby was still in the kitchen with his second pot of coffee, and he got up and went out into the yard when he heard her call.

"Look what's coming," Mother Sauls said above the wind, when Bobby arrived next to her in the yard. "It's not much, but it might get us wet. I'm going to stand out in it when it comes."

"There's a bit of an offshore wind against it," Bobby said. "It'll blow itself out before it gets here, you watch."

"I can't," she said. "I've got work to do on my writing. You watch. That's your job."

"It won't get in this far," Bobby said, but he went around to the porch of their cottage to wait for whatever did happen.

"Holler for me if it starts raining," Mother Sauls called after him, "so I can bring in my wash."

Bobby got comfortable in his tattered chair. The squall moved in closer, spreading along its black base and towering even higher. Then it blew itself out, becoming thinner, then transparent, and finally dissipating over the southern sky, as Bobby had said it would.

This, too, then, was not what he was waiting for, not the triumphant realization of Ike's prediction, nor even the long-hoped-for rain he thought might change something. Bobby tried to picture the mass arrival of the flying fish as he had imagined it before, the excitement in seeing their bodies piled in the yard; but by now there was no feeling left in this wooden fantasy. The flying fish had gone the way of Bobby's other scenarios, especially since Ike's admission that he was a fraud. But Bobby was not ready to give up on the prediction. He could not give up on it. If it wasn't flying fish, it would be something else, because he had come to believe in the power of the prediction, beyond Ike's part in it and his denial of its validity. He believed in its inevitability and could tell himself he believed in it even before Ike ever came and announced it, because without that, he knew he might as well walk out into the Gulf. He knew now that he had been waiting for years for something like Ike's flamboyant pronouncement to lift him out of the constant sameness of the Gulf, his relationship with Mother Sauls, and the unresolved affair with the woman on the ice route. There had to be more than this. Ike was an instrument of that fulfillment, whether he knew it or not. It would come from the Gulf, and they would all know something they had never known before. He had to believe.

Watching the slow dissolution of the squall, Bobby thought carefully about what had happened to him in the empty cottage. He knew the images he had experienced there were tangible expressions of his own thoughts. But he did not feel crazy or disoriented. It was more like watching his life simultaneously from two vantage points— one of them infinitely distant and the other close at hand, startlingly clear but puzzling. Resting on the porch in the face of the dissolving storm, Bobby felt his fear of the cottage giving way to a powerful anticipation of what would next present itself, coupled with the overwhelming need to tell someone about it. He got out of his chair and walked the length of the porch and back again. He could see Mother Sauls at her desk, scribbling in her yellow pad. Bobby went into the living room and stood over her shoulder.

"I'm working," she said.

"I have something to tell you," Bobby said. "I've been seeing things."

Mother Sauls put down her pencil, took off her glasses, and looked up at him. Bobby remembered her body against his in the night. He hoped she remembered too and would listen.

"What things?" she said, almost gently.

"I've been seeing things in the empty cottage," Bobby said. "The one Jim died in."

"Oh, Bobby," she said, turning away. "Not that."

"Listen to me, please," Bobby said. "It started the day Wilkes came, when I went in there to get the chairs. The living room was full of flying fish. There were hundreds of them, all piled on each other, and they were all dead. It smelled terrible. There was the smell too. It wasn't just seeing them."

She looked at him again, and there were tears in her eyes. "What else," she said.

"Not long ago I found the bedroom exactly as it was when I found Jim," Bobby said. "Only he wasn't there. The gun was, though, and everything else was the same."

Mother Sauls sighed and looked away. "Why are you telling me this?" she said.

"I could smell the blood," Bobby said. "Just like before."

"You were imagining it all."

"It was there."

Mother Sauls got up from her chair and went out to the porch. Bobby waited a moment, then followed. She was facing the water, and Bobby stood behind her, looking over her shoulder.

"What happened to the rain?" she asked after some time.

"It blew away," Bobby said. "It came close, but then it blew apart. We won't get any today."

Mother Sauls faced him, then reached out a hand and touched him on the arm, just for a moment, but long enough for Bobby's heart to leap into his throat. She gave him a rare smile, like the ones he had seen when they were very young. "You're not finally slipping away, are you?" she said.

"No," Bobby said. "I'm still here. I'm just trying to tell you some of the things that are happening."

"You're getting old," said Mother Sauls.

After a lunch during which neither of them spoke, Bobby retreated to the porch to sleep in his chair. Some time later, in the middle of a dream about salamanders and chameleons coming up the screen in a white sunlight, he was awakened by the sound of Ike's Harley in the yard. He surged from his chair, left the porch, and went into the hard, midday sun. Ike was steering the motorcycle in big, easy circles around the yard, and Mother Sauls was straddling the seat behind him in her pink shorts and billowing white blouse, her expression alternating between terror and delight. Bobby watched them circling, then hailed them as they drew close.

"What the hell are you doing?" he yelled over the deep roar of the bike.

"I'm teaching her to ride," Ike yelled back. "I'm going to take her out on the road."

"What?"

"We're going up to Tallahassee," Mother Sauls said. "I've got to get out of here for a while. You watch out for Linda. We'll be back later."

Ike waved, then gunned the motor and wheeled the Harley around. And they were gone up the yard and out onto the blacktop. Bobby stood in the sun and watched them go. Linda came waddling across the grass from her cottage and put her arm around his waist.

"Where are they off to?" she said.

"Tallahassee," Bobby answered. "Your grandmother's become a Hell's Angel."

"They'll be all right," Linda said. "Ike knows what he's doing."

"So does Mother," Bobby said, still watching the road and the little cloud of transparent gray smoke they had left. "Come on. I'm supposed to look after you. I'll fix you some iced tea, and you can keep me company."

"I was just fixing to lie down for a while," Linda said.

"You can do it at our place," Bobby said. "Come on. I'd like to have you around."

They walked arm in arm through the languid heat, up the split cypress steps, and onto Bobby's porch. "Thought it might rain earlier," Bobby said. "But it passed on. You all right? Sit down here, and I'll fix us some tea."

"Forget the tea," Linda said. "Let's just sit and talk a bit." She motioned to the chair next to her, and Bobby sat down. The Gulf was flat as a tabletop and a nearly uniform cobalt blue. There were no longer any clouds at all.

"It's Ronnie, isn't it?" Bobby said. "I knew that transformation of his wouldn't last."

"He can't help it," Linda said. "He goes back and forth so quickly in his moods, and I don't blame him. He knows."

"Did you tell him?"

"God, no," Linda said. "Do you think I'm crazy?"

"I thought at first from the way he's been acting that you had," Bobby said. "I thought you had told him and you were both starting over."

"No," Linda said. "He was just trying to pretend everything was all right. He was trying very hard."

"He was nice," Bobby said. "I liked him that way."

"He's getting crazy again because I'm a week overdue. He threatened the baby again last night and said some awful things."

"You'll have to leave," Bobby said. "We'll put you up in Tallahassee, and Mother can stay with you."

"I just can't, Granddad. Part of me wants to get as far away from him as I can, but the bigger part doesn't believe he would ever do anything to hurt me or the baby. I might be wrong, and that's what has me scared—he's got one hell of a temper—but as long as I believe he won't, I can't leave. I even keep hoping maybe he'll take off. But I know it won't be me. I love him, Granddad. Besides, I feel sorry for him. I've hurt him very much."

Bobby looked out at the Gulf and remembered how differently Mother Sauls had reacted to the discovery of his own affair with the woman on the ice route. There had been no accusations or anger, or anything at all. Only the immediate and permanent silence, the years of silence. Seeing Linda like this now, he wondered which was worse, but he knew that with the anger in the open, something would give, something would pass. Better that than the terrible hostility, pent up over so many years.

"We have to hope the baby is born with the finger," Bobby said. "That will make everything all right in the short run, and then you'll have time to find out what you should do with Ronnie."

"He isn't a bad man," Linda said, turning her red, swollen, but still-beautiful face toward Bobby. "I really think he loves me. He just doesn't know how to act in all this."

Bobby thought for a moment. "You have to give those answers," he said. "But right now you should go and rest. Go take my bed. I'll be out here, and you can call if you need anything." He stood and helped Linda to her feet, and together they walked to the bedroom. Bobby switched on the fan in the soft yellow room, and Linda stretched out on the bed.

"It won't be long now," he said. "Something will happen. I really believe everything's going to be fine."

Linda closed her eyes, and Bobby watched her, remembering the distant, expressionless stare on her little face when he had come back down to the beach with the confirmation of her father's death. Today, her world was no less complicated and perhaps held no more meaning, but she was swimming against it as hard as he was.

On the way back out to the porch, Bobby was stopped by the pile of papers on Mother Sauls's desk, and a great urge to look into them came upon him. But he did not read them then. He went to the refrigerator for a beer and then out to the porch, where he slowly drank it and had two cigarettes while looking off into the purple arc of horizon. And then he went back in, sat at the desk, and took up a stack of the papers.

"As I have related," he read,

I had known my cousin Bobby all my life but could not have told you what he looked like until the summer I was fourteen and he was sixteen. We were living in the big house in Panacea then, and Bobby's family lived a few miles north on his grandfather's farm, the old man having passed away the winter before, as I have recounted here in these pages.

The occasion was my fourteenth birthday, a Sunday, and after attending church at Shiloh, the whole family, cousins and all, returned to our place for a big "dinner on the grounds" beneath the wonderful oaks we had behind the house. It was my celebration, and while my mother fried chicken after chicken in the kitchen, and the rest of the family trickled in with their pies and potatoes and yams, I opened presents at the table under the oaks. I remember I was wearing a beautiful long white dress with purple trim about the neck and sleeves that my grandmother had made, and I had matching purple ribbons in my hair. I was very happy, and it was a beautiful day, a wonderful fall day with puffy white clouds above and cool air that smelled of wood smoke and leaves.

I opened the few simple presents from the family: a sweater my aunt Margaret had made, a box of candy, and more ribbons for my hair. And when it was over and we were finding our places to eat, Bobby approached me and said he had my present out at the front gate. I followed him out to the little wood fence in front of our house where there was a gate with an arched trellis my father had built, still covered with the confederate jasmine that had bloomed so fiercely in the summer. Bobby took my arm and led me under the trellis; he took my chin in his strong right hand and kissed me and said he hoped it was a good present, that it was all he had. My heart fell apart in a million pieces.

Bobby put the papers back in the stack on the desk and looked back over the years to the incident Mother Sauls had described. He remembered how small she had been; her tiny waist and pale narrow face, and the purple ribbons that had blown between their parting lips. He remembered the kiss and the nervous anticipation that had preceded it—about which she had known nothing. He had put one trembling hand in his pocket, hoping she wouldn't notice, but she had remembered the kiss and was kind to him in that memory.

He picked up the papers to read more but then heard Ronnie's pickup sputter into the yard. In a few moments

Junior barged into the living room. He was sunburned and sweating and looked scared.

Bobby pushed away from the desk and stood. "What are you doing back so early? It's not even four o'clock."

"Ronnie got so crazy, we couldn't work," Junior said. "He just pulled in everything, and we came back. He's in some kind of rage, Granddad."

"Where'd he go?" Bobby asked.

"Into his place, I guess," Junior said. "He was going in to yell at Linda. I told him to leave her alone, but he acted like he was going to belt me, so I shut up."

"Don't worry," Bobby said. "Linda's taking a nap here. He won't find her over there, and if he comes here, I'll take care of him."

"He's crazy," Junior said. "I'm not going out with him again."

"Good," Bobby said. "You don't have to. You can help Mother out around here."

"I'm going to take a shower," Junior said.

Bobby went out to the porch and walked to the far end so he could see Linda and Ronnie's cottage. The truck was parked in front, and the sun was blasting off the curve of windshield. For a minute Bobby heard and saw nothing. Then Ronnie came crashing out the door, threw himself into the truck, and gouged a wide swath in the grass as he peeled back out of the yard and screeched up onto the blacktop. Bobby stood watching the smoke from the tires drift away over the road, and then Linda was standing next to him.

"What was that?" she asked.

"Your crazy husband," Bobby said. "He knocked off early today and came home to raise hell."

"I'm glad I wasn't home."

"Me too," said Bobby, scratching his temple with his extra little finger. "But he isn't gone for good. He's got to come back sometime."

"I wish I'd never seen a motorcycle," said Linda. "And now Mother is out gallivanting who knows where on one of them."

Bobby didn't start worrying until after dark. He'd fixed himself and Junior some frozen pot pies for supper. Then Junior had gone surf-fishing again, and Bobby spent the evening on the porch smoking and working on a new scenario to accommodate Ike's forgotten prediction. He had grown so accustomed to the lack of conversation between them that for a long time he was not even aware Mother Sauls was not there.

His new plan for the prediction was even more ambitious than the flying fish. Like his other musings, it bloomed up from the Gulf in dreamlike fragments and gradually conformed to his will. He determined that several boats would arrive from the Gulf at the cottages; long, well-built, ancient wooden boats containing tall, bronze men with yellow hair. They would bring no provisions, tools, or weapons, nothing but knowledge, and they would move with a quiet grace. Gathered in the Saulses' yard, they would tell of their native land, an island in the Gulf no one had ever found, where there was no anger, war, envy, or guilt. Then with their perfect fingers they would touch the assembled Sauls family, and their knowledge and peace would be transmitted.

Bobby dreamed this waking dream until the light faded

from the water, and then he rose, feeling rested and quiet but brimming with excitement again, and went into the house to get a beer. The light at the desk where Mother Sauls should be was dark, and Bobby remembered she and Ike had left a long time ago. Bobby went out the front door of the cottage and looked toward the road. There were no lights in Ike's cottage or the store, just the yellow shaft of Wilkes's bare bulb spilling out onto the grass.

Bobby walked up to the road and looked down it both ways, then came back down the yard and looked in Wilkes's window. He was on the sofa, working on the skeleton. Bobby felt something well up in his belly like a soft, hot balloon. It was not like Mother Sauls to be gone so long. She never went anywhere but into Carrabelle or Panacea for fish and supplies, and then only rarely. While he worried, Bobby stood some distance from the window so he wouldn't be seen and watched Wilkes working on the skeleton. Maybe there had been an accident, or maybe they had both just left. It occurred to him now that they both might be crazy enough to stay away for some time— Ike to get away from Ronnie and Linda, and Mother Sauls because she was afraid of what he had told her he had seen in the empty cottage.

Bobby watched Wilkes concentrating on the left hand of the skeleton. He was assembling the tiny bones of the hand one at a time, painstakingly drilling each of the holes and running bits of wire through them. It took him a long time with each bone, and Bobby finally grew tired of watching. He decided to go to Linda's cottage and wait for Mother Sauls there. Wilkes had not broken his concentration on the bones for a moment.

Halfway to Linda's cottage, Bobby was intercepted by Junior running up from the beach with his surf rod on his shoulder.

"Ronnie's coming up in a skiff," Junior shouted. "And from the way he's driving that thing and carrying on, he's drunk as shit."

Bobby looked down the beach and in the tan dusk could barely make out the boat, which was bouncing and weaving about fifty yards offshore.

"Get in the house and stay with Linda," he said. "I'll stay out here."

Junior leaned his rod against the house and went inside. Bobby stood where he was and watched the boat make a wide circle directly out from the cottages, then head straight into the beach. Ronnie steered standing up, and when he ran the boat up on the sand, the impact nearly threw him out.

"Son of a bitch," Ronnie swore. He straightened himself, staggered out of the boat, and stood swaying in the sand.

"Where's the whore?" he shouted. "Hey, Linda. Can you hear me, bitch?"

Linda and Junior came out onto her porch. "Bobby, he's drunk," Linda said.

"Yes," said Bobby. "He is."

"You'd better come inside."

"No," Bobby replied. "I'm all right. He won't do anything."

"He's been crazy all day," Junior warned. "I was with him."

"He's been crazy a lot longer than that," Bobby said. "But he's just drunk now. Go back inside."

"Goddamn whore," Ronnie shouted. "I know you can hear me. How's it feel to be a goddamn tramp, huh? How's it feel?"

"Should I go to him?" Linda said. She was beginning to cry, but her voice was strong.

"No. I'll talk to him," Bobby said, and started down to the beach.

"Be careful, Granddad," said Linda.

Ronnie was leaning against the skiff when Bobby got to him. He was sweating profusely, and his eyes were glazed and mean. He lurched away from the boat when he saw Bobby and fell on his seat in the water and stayed there. Bobby saw his eyes soften with the fall into the water.

"Hey, old man," he said, "how's the bitch?"

"Stop that kind of talk," Bobby said, "and get on out of here. You're just making things worse for everybody."

"I'll leave when I'm ready," Ronnie snarled.

"Get ready, then. It's late. We all have to go to bed."

"I'm tired," Ronnie said.

"So, go on, then. You can't stay here tonight."

"I won't stay here again, *ever*. Not now." He tried to get up from the water, but couldn't.

"If it was up to me, you wouldn't," Bobby said. "But it isn't. I'm just telling you to get out of here now."

"I can't," Ronnie said.

"Why not?"

"I can't get up, dammit. Give me a hand."

"Will you leave?"

"Yes. Help me up."

Bobby reached down and pulled him to his feet. Ronnie

swayed for a moment, then grabbed the side of the boat
again.

"I got a right," he said.

"No you don't," said Bobby. "Not like this."

"I'm fucked up." Ronnie laughed. "I hope I can drive
this thing." He climbed into the boat and fell heavily into
the seat.

"Not like that," Bobby said. "We'll have to push it off
the beach first."

Ronnie got back out and held on to the side of the skiff.

"Come on, help me push," Bobby said.

"Wait a minute." Ronnie grinned. "I have to fart." He
reached in his shirt pocket and pulled out a lighter.

"What the hell are you doing?" Bobby said. "Give me
that."

Ronnie yanked his hand away, bent over, and lit the
lighter near his rear end and farted long and loud. There
was a flash of light, and Ronnie fell down laughing. "I
haven't done that in a long time," he said. "You ever light
farts, old man?"

"No," Bobby said. "I don't fart anymore, and I only
shit once a month. Get up. You can't be bothering people
like this. Get on out of here and straighten up."

Bobby helped Ronnie to his feet once more. Together
they pushed the boat until it floated, then Ronnie climbed
in again, and Bobby gave it another shove. With Ronnie
slumped over the wheel, Bobby watched the skiff drift
into the silver moonlight that was broken into millions of
jumping blades on the water's surface. Then he turned
away and didn't hear the motor start until he was back
on his own porch, with the first of a long series of beers
and cigarettes.

There were no real waves to speak of on that part of the coast. But there was the lapping sound the Gulf made on the beach as it moved in its giant bowl and the night sounds in the trees, palmettos, and grass around the cottage—sounds real and imagined, past and present. Bobby sat in his chair on the porch and closed his eyes—not to sleep, but to follow the sounds. He listened to the water's broken sound and then, through palmetto fronds, to the long, dark, droning tunnel of the cicadas that was the amplified sound of heat. Bobby followed the vibrating sounds to the treetops, where the wind moved gently and occasionally through the pines. The sudden and nearby sound of a whippoorwill brought a profound and perfect sadness, and he stayed in it until the sound of a motorcycle turning off the road into the yard pulled him free.

Bobby waited until he heard her open the front screen door, and then he got up and went into the kitchen. Mother Sauls was pouring herself a glass of milk.

"I hope you didn't worry," she said without looking at him. "We just rode all over. It was great fun. Have you ever ridden on one of those things?" She was wiping the counter and all the appliances, and being too busy the way she always got when she was anxious.

"Once," Bobby said. "A long time ago. And I *was* worried. I didn't think you'd be gone this long."

"Well, I'm sorry," she said. "But I feel great for having done it." She finished the milk and washed out the glass in the sink. "Did anything happen here while I was gone?"

"No," Bobby said. "Except that I heard a whippoorwill outside a while ago. I haven't heard one all summer."

"There aren't as many as there used to be," said Mother Sauls. "We used to hear half a dozen a night, all calling at once, remember?"

"And fireflies," Bobby said. "There aren't any more fireflies, either. I don't know what's happening."

"Maybe the world is stopping," Mother Sauls said with a smile. "Running out of things to show us. Are you coming to bed?"

"In a few minutes," Bobby said.

One of the practical benefits of unfiltered cigarettes and strong, black coffee was made manifest every morning in the little bathroom that stood like an afterthought at the back of the cottage, with its own window looking out onto the Gulf. There, in spite of his visions, dreams, and persistent belief in a psychic prediction whose perpetrator denounced it, Bobby Sauls sat and considered himself to be a practical man, as he had all his life. He was remembering when he was eleven years old, when he'd decided the extra little finger he carried on his right hand was of no use, and he'd determined to remove it, one way or another. On a cold January morning, as he was splitting and stacking a cord of wood with his brother, Jack, behind their father's barn, he'd announced his intentions and tried to enlist Jack's help.

"I want you to cut this son of a bitch off," Bobby said. "I'm sick of it. I'll just lay it up on the stump, and you whack it off with the ax."

Jack looked at him with the ax poised over a two-foot piece of oak. "I'd do it in a minute," Jack said, "but Daddy'll kill me when he finds out. Why don't you do it yourself?"

"I don't think I can," Bobby said. "It'd be better if you did it."

"I can't," Jack said again. "Not with the ax. It would end up taking them both off, and then you'd only have four. That'd be worse than having six."

"Give me your knife, then," Bobby said. "I'll saw it off."

Jack took out his pocketknife, opened it, and handed it to Bobby. "You'll have to cut through the flap of skin first," Jack said, "before you can think about getting through the bone. There's going to be a lot of blood."

Bobby took the knife and put his hand palm down on the chopping stump, spreading his fingers as wide as he could. The two little fingers were nearly as one. "You sop up the blood," he said.

"Better have something to bite on," Jack said. "It's likely to hurt some too." He took off his thick leather belt, and Bobby put it between his teeth. He put the knife to the flap of skin between the fingers.

"Go on," Jack said.

"Ah mam," Bobby mumbled through the belt.

"Shit," Jack said. "You ain't cutting anything. Go ahead."

Bobby started the knife down through the skin, and the blood came up before the pain. And then their father came around the corner of the barn and saw them. He stopped in his tracks for a second and then he charged Bobby, knocking him away from the stump, and then he carried straight on to Jack and threw him up against the barn.

"Damn, Daddy," Jack cried. "I didn't do nothing."

"What the hell are y'all doing," the man yelled. He let go of Jack and turned to Bobby, who was still holding the knife in his hand and clenching the belt in his teeth. Bobby just stood looking at his father. Then the man yanked the belt from his mouth, and Bobby followed, ending up inches from his father's face.

"I'm going to cut it off," Bobby said bravely. "I'm sick of it."

"The hell you are," the man said. "Give me that knife."

Bobby handed it over, and his father folded it and put it in his pocket. "You keep chopping," he said to Jack. "And you come with me." He turned and started away to the woods, swinging the belt at his side. Bobby looked once at Jack, who shrugged and set up another piece of oak on the stump. Bobby gave up and followed his father.

There was a path beginning at the back of the barn that led down through the woods a quarter mile to a narrow stream that fed into the Ochlockonee River. Bobby watched his father's broad, determined back moving several yards ahead on the sandy trail through the dappled shadows cast by the pale sun through the trees. He decided he would take his punishment without a sound in order to show the man how determined he was to remove the finger. He hated it. It served no useful purpose, and he was tired of being teased about it by the other boys.

His father had stopped by the stream and was waiting, looking down into the moving water, waving the belt loosely along his leg. Bobby moved to his side and waited too. Some patches of mud along the bank that the sun had not found were still frozen from the frost that had come for two nights running, but the stream itself moved swiftly and was the color of heavily creamed coffee. Bobby watched it run and waited. In a few minutes his father rolled up the belt and put it in his pocket. He took out his handkerchief and pressed it to Bobby's hand, between the fingers where it was still bleeding. Then he looked Bobby straight in the eye, and the anger was gone.

"You don't want to lose that finger," he said. "You want to be proud of it, Son."

"I'm not."

"It means you're a Sauls."

"Wouldn't I be a Sauls without it?"

"Not as much of one," his father said. "It means something special."

"What? That we're freaks?"

His father took his time replying. He was looking down into the water again. The sun was climbing through the trees across the stream into a clear, blue sky. "It's a sign of love and devotion," the man said. Bobby kicked in the dirt with the toe of his boot. "It shows that I took the right woman for my wife. The finger is a sign from God, and you should be proud of it. God wants us to keep the family close, not to marry outside it. If we did, we'd lose the finger, and God might get mad then." He looked up into Bobby's eyes again. "I reckon cutting it off would make God even madder, don't you?"

Bobby did not answer for some time. He was watching the coffee stream running down into the woods, where overhanging branches made a dark, narrow tunnel and where he knew the smell of wet, molding leaves hung so thick you could taste it.

"I ain't giving no kid of mine this damn thing," Bobby said. "No matter what God thinks. It's a curse." He looked

straight at his father and felt momentarily dizzy with ex-
hilaration from standing up to him. "You can stop me
now," he said. "But you won't always be around, and one
of these days I'll get rid of it. I ain't stupid, you know."

"Maybe not," his father said evenly, taking the belt from
his pocket and unrolling it. "But by the time you're able
to sit again, you'll think you are."

Still sitting on the toilet in the stifling afternoon, Bobby
remembered the beating and his father's warning about
the finger. He had been right, there was no getting away
from it. He had married in the family the same as his
father and grandfather before him, and now he was twelve
years older than his father had been when he died, but he
still felt like the boy being lectured at the stream. It had
been practical to marry Mother Sauls: she was there, and
she was the same as he. It had been practical to work in
the oyster boats and to buy the cottages and a hundred
other things. What had not been practical or sensible was
the woman on the ice route and the way she loved his
extra little finger.

Bobby lit a Camel and the smoke went nowhere in the
chipped, black-and-white tiled cubicle. It was not worth
thinking about, the way she had loved the finger, but it
came anyway, and he had long since forgotten, if he ever
knew, how to stop those things from coming.

Sometimes she would put the finger in her mouth, beginning with the nail, then isolate it from its twin with
her teeth as she worked her way along it, sucking it until
there was pain and Bobby had to tell her to stop. That
was only one of several creative functions she came up

with for the finger, but it was her favorite, and she always returned to it when they were lying in bed in the last few minutes before he had to get back on the ice route. Bobby would sometimes be nearly asleep in the warm morning room with the sun just beginning to come up the wall at the head of the bed, and she would be very gentle with his finger, caressing it with her tongue until he was fully awake and then aroused. But then it was time for him to leave and it was for what seemed like a long time. It was one of her ways of bringing him back.

Bobby finished his constitutional, flushed, and left the bathroom. Mother Sauls had gone up to open the store, and Junior was on the porch reading a comic book. Bobby watched his grandson's silent concentration in the long, lulling heat of the porch and then went and sat in his own chair next to Junior.

"Let's do something," Bobby said.

Junior laid the comic book in his lap. "Like what?"

"Want to fish a little?"

"It's too hot," Junior said. "You know that. We'd have to go to deep water to catch anything, and I'm not up for that."

"Let's take a ride somewhere, then. Let's go over to Panama City and look at the girls."

"Too far," Junior said. "We'd melt getting there."

"Well, goddammit," Bobby said. "Let's go swimming, then. I haven't been in the water in a long time."

"All right," Junior said. "I'll do that. Let me get on my suit."

"Good," Bobby said. "We'll swim, and then I'll fix us some fish sandwiches and cold beer for lunch."

Junior scrambled out of his chair and disappeared into

the house. Bobby eased himself to his feet and slowly made his way to his bedroom and put on the only bathing suit he had owned in thirty years. It had started out being blue, but was now a light gray with all the elastic shot, and it only stayed up with the strings firmly tied. Bobby took the cigarette pack from his shirt, got a towel from the bathroom, and went to meet Junior on the porch. The Gulf was flat and blue, and as they made their way down the path through the palmettos, Bobby could see some mullet jumping not far offshore, hurling their stiff, silver bodies from the water in leap after leap, making a noise like a hand slapping the water.

"Looks like something's feeding, Junior," Bobby said. "Something's after the mullet."

"They just jump that way for the hell of it, don't they, Granddad?"

"Sometimes," Bobby said. "But not that last one. He was coming out too fast. Something was after him. Don't go out too far." He put his towel and cigarettes down on the sand and followed Junior down the beach and into the Gulf. Although it must have been eighty-five degrees in the water, it felt cool because the air was so much warmer. Bobby walked in until he was waist-deep, and then he eased down until only his head was out.

"Ah," he said. "We ought to do this every day."

"It's too much trouble," Junior said. "It's so easy, we never get to it. You know what I mean?"

"Yes," Bobby said. "There are lots of things like that."

Junior was floating on his back with his arms out crucifixation style, staring up at the sky. It gave Bobby a funny feeling and he turned away and looked at the cottages up on the shore, shining white in the sun. He could see Ike crossing the yard to Linda's place. Bobby waved, but Ike wasn't looking.

"Do you ever wish you didn't have the finger?" Bobby asked the still-floating Junior.

"I don't think about it," Junior said. "Not much, anyway. A teacher at school said it was no different than a birthmark. We have a kid there who has a big brown blotch over one-half of his face. It's not as bad as that."

"I guess not," Bobby said. "I've just been thinking about it today. I tried to cut mine off once, you know."

Junior came out of his float and stood looking at him. "You did? Why?"

"I hated it," Bobby said. "But then I forgot about it a long time, and when Jim was born with it, I was happy, I guess."

Junior was dunking himself up and down in the water. "I'm used to it," he said when he bobbed up to stay.

Bobby looked up and down the beach. It was a beautiful, sparkling day, and it felt good to be in the water and not thinking about anything. Ike came out of Linda's cottage, and this time he looked out at the water and waved, but he kept going down the yard. Bobby watched him all the way into his cottage up by the road.

Junior was swimming away from him, parallel to the beach, his long arms coming in and out of the water like a spider escaping some predator. Bobby watched him swim for fifty yards and then turn around and start back. He swam twenty or so yards and then suddenly stopped and stood frozen in water that came up to his chest and called out to Bobby.

"Something big bumped me," he said. "It was huge. I didn't see it but I felt it go by."

"Get out now," Bobby yelled, remembering the frantic leaps of the mullet. Junior broke for the beach and made it in a flurry of elbows and knees. Then Bobby saw the long, brownish shape of the hammerhead in the shallow water between himself and the beach. It was swimming along the same route Junior had taken, and it was at least seven feet long.

"There it is, Granddad," Junior yelled. "It's a big hammerhead."

"I see it," Bobby called. "You just stay where you are. He doesn't know I'm here yet." Bobby watched the big fish moving slowly with the shore, and then something seemed to startle it. It darted away from the beach, and Bobby started carefully in, trying not to make even a ripple. But the shark turned and came back through the water between him and the beach, and Bobby froze. The hammerhead swam for a few yards, then turned again, coming even closer. Bobby got a good look at his wide, ugly head before it turned out toward deeper water, some fifteen yards from him. Slowly, Bobby started in again, watching the big fish all the while.

When he was still twenty yards from shore, he saw the shark swing around toward him, and he started running through the knee-deep water. Junior came out and grabbed him under the arms and dragged him the last few feet up onto the sand, where he collapsed in a breathless, aching heap and turned to see the hammerhead glide by in water that was barely deep enough to hold him, then head out and disappear in the water beyond the sandbar.

"Shit," Junior said. "That was close."

"Naw," Bobby panted. "He wasn't really after us. He was after mullet and was just clearing us out. If he'd wanted you, he'd have done more than bump you." It was not the first time he had been in the water with sharks, but it was the first time he hadn't been scared, and he did not know the reason for that. It had all been so removed and distant, like watching a movie, but he had done what he needed to do.

"Jesus, he was a big sucker, though," said Junior.

"Yes, he was," Bobby said thoughtfully. "I guess we'd better stay out of the water awhile. Let's go have that beer." When he stood and hooked the towel around the back of his neck and looked out at the horizon, he was already forgetting the big shark. He was thinking that if he had gone ahead and cut off the finger when he was eleven, it was likely that nothing since then would have happened the way it did.

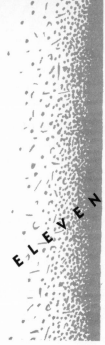

ELEVEN

As soon as it was light enough to see, Bobby walked up the yard and got his fishing tackle from the back room of the store and put it in the car parked in front. He went back for some beer, crackers and cheese, and Vienna sausage, and then he went to Ike's bedroom window and rattled the screen. There was no response.

"Let's go, ape-man," Bobby said through the screen. "We're going fishing."

"Go away," Ike groaned.

"Come on, you owe me. Remember?"

"I remember, asshole. Let's do it some other time."

"Now," Bobby said. "I've got everything ready. Get your butt up, or I'll burn the place down around you."

"Do it," Ike said. "I'm sleeping."

Bobby gave up on the window, went around to the porch, and let himself in. Ike was sprawled facedown on the bed like so many sacks of fertilizer. Bobby pulled on one massive foot, and Ike cursed. "Goddammit, I'm coming," he said. "Give me a minute." He rolled over and sat up on the side of the bed. "Why we have to go in the middle of the night is beyond me. What a shitty time to go fishing."

"It's the best time," Bobby said. "We're already late. I'll wait for you in the car." He went out into the gray light and stood against the car. Ike came out in ten minutes, wearing his Levi's, boots, and a black tee shirt.

"You're going to die out there," Bobby said. "Why do you always wear that same shit?"

"What about your little uniform," Ike growled, scratching his voluminous beard. "I've never seen you in anything else either."

Bobby was in his customary khaki shorts, white tee shirt, and tan cap with the crossed anchors. "Mine's more practical," he said.

"Fuck practical," Ike said.

Ike got in the car and closed his eyes, and Bobby drove the few miles to the marina on the Ochlockonee Bay, where he kept the fishing boat. He parked under some oak trees trailing Spanish moss, and Ike helped him carry the gear down to the water. The boat was a seventeen-foot open fisherman with a center console, several years old but well maintained and seaworthy, with a seventy-horse outboard motor. But Ike eyed it warily.

"It's not very big," he said.

"It's plenty," Bobby said. "Get in. We've got to fill the tanks."

Bobby got in after Ike and started the motor, then idled down the marina to the gas pumps, and topped off the two cans in the boat. In a few minutes they were up on plane in the river channel heading to the open Gulf. Ike sat on the bench in front of the console. "That's where we're going," Bobby shouted over the motor. "Straight out. There's something I want to show you."

"How far?" said Ike.

"About seven miles. You'll love it. We'll troll a little on the way out, for mackerel, although it's probably too late in the year for them, and then we'll try the flats on the way back in."

They cleared the mouth of the bay. The land fell away quickly on either side, and they were in the Gulf. The water almost immediately took on a clear, greenish hue with brilliant white foam where they plowed through. It stayed that way for a half hour and then became bluer with long shafts of sunlight stabbing down when they reached deeper water. Bobby eased back on the throttle, and the bow of the boat came gently down. There was no rush. And it felt good to be back on the water. There was a slight chop that grew into a bigger swell as they got farther out, but the boat took it easily, and Bobby stood with his feet spread at the wheel and felt very young.

Ike stuck his head around the windscreen. "What unit was your boy with in the Nam?" he said.

"I don't remember," Bobby said. "It was a long time ago. He was around Da Nang a lot, I remember that, and then out in the bush for months at a time."

"Yeah, me too," Ike said. "How'd he do? Did he make it?"

"He came back," Bobby said, steering around a clump of floating seaweed. "But he blew his head off with a shotgun not long after. Right there in one of the cottages not far from yours. He had a wife and everything, but she took off right after. We kept the kids and haven't seen her since. Junior still thinks he was killed in the war, but Linda knows. She remembers."

"I've heard a lot of guys did that," Ike said. "I guess it was just too much for him, huh?"

"He should have left his body over there," Bobby said. "That's where he died. But that was a long time ago too. Let's do some fishing, all right?" He put the motor in neutral, then eased it out again so it was doing a slow troll.

"Come on back and take the wheel a minute," he said. "I want to put out some lines."

Ike came around the console with some difficulty. He couldn't seem to find a way to stand without being thrown off balance by the gentle swell. "What do I do?" he asked.

"Just keep it right where it is," Bobby said. "I'll only be a few minutes."

"How come it's rolling so much? It wasn't doing that when we were going fast."

Bobby laughed. "That's because we were cutting through the swell," he said. "But it's got hold of us now. Don't worry, it's only two or three feet. I've been out in much worse. This is really pretty calm."

"Not to me, it's not," Ike said.

"If you get sick, go to the side," Bobby said. "Don't mess up the boat. It's hell to get out, and the guy that does it is the guy that cleans it up. That's one of the laws of the sea."

He went back and took the two spinning rods from their holders. On one he rigged a silver spoon, and on the other, a yellow feather duster, both on wire leaders. He threw the two lines out about forty yards behind the boat and fixed the rods off the stern in PVC holders, so they were angled up and out. While he was setting the drag on the reels he felt the boat turning in a wide circle, then tossing more violently as the swell hit them broadside. He looked forward and saw Ike over the side, vomiting up everything but his shoelaces. Bobby took the wheel and put the boat back on course.

"Good boy," he said. "Get it over with now. You'll be all right after this."

But Ike had to go over the side twice more while they trolled slowly through the blue water without a strike. When there was nothing more to bring up, he dipped his face in the water to clean out his beard and came up dripping and cursing like an angry Neptune.

"Goddamn," he said. "You didn't mention this part."

"Didn't think to." Bobby laughed. "It never happens to me. You all right now?"

"Better," Ike said. "But I'm taking care of this right now." He reached in his hip pocket and took out his black leather wallet, which was connected to his belt by a little chain, and produced what looked like a flattened, home-made cigarette.

"This is supposed to be good for nausea," he said. "But I've never used it for that."

"What the hell is it?"

"Pot," Ike declared. "Weed, Mary Jane, reefer, dope. Don't tell me you've never tried it?"

Bobby went aft and started reeling in the lines. "Never," he said. "I want to keep my wits about me."

"Haw," Ike bellowed, standing with his feet spread on the deck. "You've never had any wits. Gimme your lighter, old man. I'll fix you."

Bobby finished with the rods and put them back in

their holders along the gunwale. He took his lighter from his pocket and handed it to Ike at the console. "Here," Bobby said. "Smoke your brains out, but not me."

Ike lit the joint and inhaled forever into his huge lungs. After about a minute he let out his breath and held out the joint to Bobby. "Come on, man," he said. "For me. It's not like you think. You'll feel just fine."

"What if I can't drive the boat?" Bobby said.

"Well I sure as hell can't." Ike laughed. "You'll be great. You'll drive it like you've never driven it before. Come on. I wouldn't steer you wrong."

Bobby took the joint and dragged on it like it was one of his Camels.

"Not like that, man," Ike said. "You have to hold it in your lungs awhile. Try it again."

Bobby took another drag and held it as long as he could, then blew out the smoke and started the boat motor. "Nothing," he said. "Beer's a lot better. Always has been, always will be." He pushed the throttle forward, and Ike nearly fell out. He grabbed the rail on the console and held on.

"One more," Ike said, steadying himself as the boat went up on plane. "One more."

Bobby took it from him and inhaled deeply, then concentrated on the water ahead. He was looking at the sheen of light on the water. It moved with each swell like a flexible skin.

"What are you grinning for, man?" Ike said after a short time.

"I'm not."

"The hell you're not. You're stoned, man."

Against his will Bobby felt the smile coming across his

whole face. The Gulf was beautiful, alive and interacting with the sunlight as he had never seen it before, and the spray coming off the bow was gold and silver and excruciatingly slow in falling. He felt euphoric and in command of the whole ocean. Perhaps there was something to Ike's medicine after all.

"There you go," Ike shouted. "I'm cured, and you're stoned."

Bobby flew at the helm of the boat for ten minutes, and then two porpoises suddenly appeared on either side of the bow, one nearly black and the other dappled like an Appaloosa, rolling and racing just ahead of the speeding boat.

"Holy shit," Ike shouted. "What are those?"

"Porpoises." Bobby laughed. "They're playing."

"Beautiful," Ike said. "Just beautiful."

"If we're lucky we'll see some flying fish," Bobby said. He started weaving the boat in a long zigzag pattern, and the porpoises stayed right with them for a few minutes. Then suddenly they were gone, and the men were alone again on the wide, clear, brilliant expanse of water.

"Unbelievable," Ike said.

Bobby spotted the marker buoy he was looking for, then turned on a new course to the east for ten minutes, slowed to trolling speed again, and carefully scanned the water ahead. The wind had died some, and the seas were nearly calm. When he saw the slight boil ahead on the surface, he cut the motor and they drifted in.

"What are we doing?" Ike asked. He had been quiet since the porpoises, gripping the handrail on the console and looking out at the sea.

"I want to show you something you'll never forget,"

Bobby said. "Look at the water." They had drifted in over the boil, and the water was clear as a bath. Bobby looked over the side and could see all the way to the sandy bottom, some twenty feet down.

"What is it?" Ike said.

"A freshwater spring," Bobby said. "Isn't it amazing? Throw out the anchor. We're going to stay awhile."

Ike worked his way forward on his hands and knees and let out the anchor rope, then came back to the console. Bobby was rigging one of the rods with a simple weight and hook.

"How can that be?" Ike said. "We're way out in the fucking ocean."

"It's an underground river, I guess," Bobby said. "And it just comes up out here. I don't know. But it's been out here as long as I can remember." He finished with the rod, opened one of the cans of Vienna sausage and broke off a chunk to fix to the hook. "There isn't much to it," he said. "It's only about twenty yards across, but it pumps pure, fresh water." He put the sausage on the hook and threw the line over the side. Ike looked down into the bubbling water.

"Can you drink it?" Ike asked.

"Sure. Get yourself a cup of it. There's some under the console there."

Ike got a cup and dipped it over the side. He sipped tentatively and then pronounced it wonderful. "It's better than the water at the cottages," he said. "Unbelievable."

Bobby's rod tip jerked down, and he started reeling in. They could see a fat bluegill rising slowly in the clear water, and in a minute Bobby had it in the boat. "This is a freshwater fish," Bobby said. "Best fishing hole I know of. I guess they came out here through the underground river, and there's always been a mess of them. They don't go anywhere because they can't live outside in the salt water, and nothing comes into the fresh water to wipe them out. Pretty neat, huh?" He took the bluegill off the hook and held it up to Ike, then gently placed it back in the water.

"None of the big fish come in to eat them?" Ike said.

"Every now and then, I guess," Bobby said. "But they'll die if they stay too long, and I suppose fish know about things like that."

"So they've got their own little pond out here in the middle of the Gulf," Ike said. "They can't leave it, and nothing else can come in."

"Not for long," said Bobby.

"Damn," Ike said. "That's pretty heavy."

Bobby went to the cooler and got them each a beer. "That's it," he said. They stood and looked into the spring a long time while they drank the beer, and then Ike laughed and poked Bobby in the ribs.

"You like that dope, don't you, old man?" He laughed. "You're making all this up, aren't you?"

"It's all right," Bobby said. "Beer's still better, and no, this is really happening. This really is a freshwater spring."

"You ought to turn on your old lady," Ike said. "It might loosen her up."

"She'd never do it," Bobby said, staring into the water. "It probably wouldn't work on her, anyway."

"What's that all about?" Ike said. "She runs you around like a bad stepchild. I wouldn't put up with it myself."

"You might," Bobby said. "If there was a reason."

"What's the reason?"

"It's an old story," Bobby said, and for the first time he knew he was going to tell someone that story. He suddenly felt light-headed.

Ike sat in the bottom of the boat with his back against the gunwale and took another beer from the cooler. "I'm listening," he said.

Bobby sat down in the swivel seat at the console and looked out at the horizon. "When I was twenty or twenty-one, my brother, Jack, and I started an ice route down along the coast," he began. "We had an old truck, and we built an icebox on the back, got fifty-pound blocks at a place in Tallahassee, and worked the little towns and stores between St. Marks and Carrabelle. We did real good, and after about a year we got another truck and split up the route. Jack took the customers closer in to Tallahassee, and I got the coast route.

"There was this one place—a store owned by a fisherman named Simmons down at St. Marks—I used to go to every Tuesday and Thursday. Simmons would go out fishing every morning, and his wife ran the store. She was the one I did business with. Well, she started having fresh coffee waiting for me when I got there, and then one thing led to another, and we got involved."

"What do you mean, involved?" Ike asked.

"You know, personal," Bobby said.

"What?"

"Sex, goddammit. We started having sex."

"Oh." Ike laughed. "That's good."

"It was," Bobby said. "It was wonderful. I was young and strong and thought I could do anything. Mother and I had been married about a year, and it used to bother me that I was meeting this woman. But she was very beautiful, and every time I got there with her I forgot everything else. It went on that way for seven or eight months."

"How did Mother find out?"

"One morning I got there with the ice and took it into the store, and we went back into her kitchen like we always did. Their house was on the back of the store, and her bedroom was on the back of the house, looking out at the mouth of the river. That morning, though, we never made it to the bedroom. We were so excited, we just started undressing right there in the kitchen, and for some reason, I stuck her panties in my back pocket. I guess I was thinking I didn't want any evidence lying around for her husband to find, but I stuck them there and forgot about it."

"Oh shit," Ike said. "And Mother found them?"

"Mother found them," Bobby said. "Doing the wash. She always laid my clean clothes out on the bed every morning, just like she does now. And a couple of days later, when I went in to get dressed after having my coffee, there were my clothes, all laid out neat and clean, and there were the panties right alongside. I almost shit right there, because I knew she knew. And I sat there on the bed a long time trying to think of what to say when she asked me about it, but she never did."

"She never asked you about it?"

"Never," Bobby said. "Even to this day. She never said a word, and to anybody looking in, it looked like nothing had changed, but see, *everything* had."

"You got off good," Ike said, reaching for another beer.

"No," Bobby said. "It turned everything upside down. She never said anything, but it was there hanging over me all the time. It still is. It's the worst thing she could have done. I'd of much rather had a fight about it, or even had her throw me out. We could have gotten over that, but she never said a word. She just kind of took charge with that silence of hers and it's been like that ever since, and I've never known what to do about it." Bobby looked down at the soft bubbling on the surface of the spring and then deeper into the water, where he could see the indistinct shapes of the panfish circling in their clear, freshwater prison.

"I'm sorry," Ike said. "Nobody deserves that."

"I do," Bobby said. "She was carrying Jim at the time."

When they left the freshwater spring it was late afternoon. The marijuana had worn off, and in its place Bobby felt a deep and pervasive melancholy that precluded any movement or conversation. He was content to watch the water and horizon, as, apparently, was Ike, each alone with his thoughts with no land in sight. They had something to eat and a beer each, and then they watched the buildup of a great mass of clouds over the mainland to the east, away from where the cottages were situated. Bobby wanted to stay on the water in case it rained, to feel the cool sting of the rain on his face, for the rejuvenation he believed it would bring. But when it didn't come, he told Ike to pull up the anchor, and they started back under half throttle. Bobby steered back by the compass, and when they could see land again and then the inlet of the bay, he picked out a particular clump of trees at the mouth of the river and gave the wheel over to Ike, telling him to keep the trees just to the right of the bow going in. Ike took the wheel and steered, grim-faced and silent, while Bobby went forward and sat with his legs dangling on either side of the bow. When they were still two miles from land he knew they were too close in for there to be any flying fish, and he gave up waiting for them to show. Instead, he watched the tireless and perfect slice of the bow through the azure water.

TWELVE

When he took her the three fifty-pound blocks of ice for the last time, it had been raining—a long, drizzling rain that had begun before dawn that morning and fell in the pines and palmettos along the narrow road to the coast with a sound like air escaping from a punctured lung. In the truck Bobby had pictured the way the rain would look from her bedroom window, on the brown marsh grass around the silent river, and the sound it would make on the roof and windows, but he did not go into the house at all. When she met him at the door of the store with the first block of ice gripped in the great claw calipers on his shoulders, she was smiling, and Bobby could smell the coffee from the kitchen. That almost made him fail, but he said nothing. And on his way out for the rest of the ice he found her standing in the rain by the truck, blocking his way.

"Aren't you coming in?" she said, and when Bobby did not answer, she moved aside. And he took in the second and then the third block of ice, and when he left she was still standing in the rain outside the store and he had said nothing.

Bobby remembered the rain and that there had been a great thickness in his chest and throat, but nothing anymore of what either had really felt like. He remembered the long drive back to Tallahassee to return the truck and that on the next morning he had started in the oyster boats to keep her from his mind. But now, on the porch of his cottage, in the first lavender light of the day it would finally rain again, he was remembering most clearly the bewilderment on her glistening face as she stood there by the truck, because he had said nothing.

In the years since, he had many times rehearsed what he should have said, what he wanted to say, and once, years later, he found himself face-to-face with her on a raw November afternoon at a tent revival a few miles from St. Marks. But again he said nothing, and they passed each other with the barest locking of eyes. Mother Sauls carried and gave birth to Jim, but there were no more children, chiefly because all opportunity for their conception was strictly controlled by her. Then as now the act was consummated at her instigation, rarely and in name only. There was no lovemaking, and Bobby slowly and surely sank into the acceptance of his punishment, so surely, that even when he was away at the CCC camp, many miles back in the woods, when women found their way to the camp on Saturday nights, he stayed in his cabin alone or walked along the black river there until fatigue took him and he could sleep without knowing his dreams.

Bobby looked at the awakening Gulf and pushed the woman from his mind with a brush of his hand down his bare leg. He stood and the pain shot through his knees, but he hobbled to the screen door and down the porch steps, and when he rounded the corner of the cottage and started up the yard, he was striding normally.

Wilkes was sitting on his own porch, facing the Gulf, and when Bobby drew near, Wilkes called to him softly.

"Good morning," said Bobby. "I didn't think anybody was up." He opened Wilkes's screen and went onto the porch. Wilkes was sitting in a wicker chair that was in worse shape than Bobby's, and he was drinking from a huge mug of coffee. He smiled benevolently at Bobby and offered a chair next to his own.

"Got any more coffee?" Bobby asked.

"Help yourself," said Wilkes. "It's in the kitchen. There are cups in the cabinet above."

"Thanks," Bobby said. "I can't seem to get enough coffee in the mornings anymore." He went into the kitchen and poured the coffee. He could see the box of bones on the table in the living room. The coffee was very good, better than his own. He returned and sat next to Wilkes. "I'm always up early," he said.

"I know," Wilkes said. "I see you out and about a lot. You must not sleep well."

"Well enough," Bobby said, "for an old man. I don't want to miss anything." He took out a Camel and offered the pack to Wilkes, who shook his head no. Bobby lit the cigarette and blew the first smoke out through his nose.

"It's going to rain today, I think," Wilkes said. "Look how early the clouds are coming. Maybe there's a storm out there."

"No," Bobby said, "it won't rain. I'd smell it if it was going to rain."

"Maybe," said Wilkes, and Bobby took that to mean that it probably did not matter to him one way or the other. They sat a long time, drinking their coffee and looking at the water. It was becoming rough, and there were actually small waves breaking out on the sandbar fifty yards off the beach. But the morning was coming up hot and still, and Bobby did not smell rain. He thought about the arrangement of bones in the box on the coffee table.

"Can I watch you work a little? I won't be any trouble."

"I suppose," Wilkes said. "There isn't much to see, though."

"Well, I'm old and there isn't much to do," Bobby said, "except wait for Linda's baby to come—and Ike's prediction."

"You believe something's really going to happen, don't you."

"Yes," Bobby said. "It has to. Life's too hard, too damn tedious. I just can't believe we live our whole lives not knowing any more than we do. It doesn't make any sense."

Wilkes stood and smiled down at Bobby. "Come on," he said. "Let's get to work. I'd enjoy your company. I'll even put on more coffee."

When they were settled in the living room, Wilkes on the sofa behind the table and Bobby across from him in a homemade rocker, with another cup of coffee, Wilkes gingerly took the partially completed skeleton from its box, cradled it in the crook of his left arm, and retrieved the remaining bones in their pillowcase from under the table. These he gently spilled onto the tabletop and spread out with his right hand, arranging the tiny hand and foot bones in separate groups, and then he laid down the skeleton and took up his small hand-operated drill. He was completing the fingers of the right hand, which looked to Bobby like the delicate, angelic remains of a raccoon forepaw he had once found in a trap near his grandfather's farm. He watched with a concentration he didn't know he possessed while the room grew yellow and warm and then closed into a soft tunnel of fascination between him and Wilkes. He wished the others could be in there to watch as well.

"You should have been a surgeon," Bobby said after some time.

"I studied anatomy books for two solid months before I started this," Wilkes said. "I know these bones better than a surgeon." Bobby watched him attach the tip of a finger, completing the assembly with a twist of the tiny wire.

"What happened?" Bobby said. "Why is it in pieces like that?"

"He was killed by dogs," Wilkes said matter-of-factly, looking up. "My wife was hanging clothes outside where we lived, in the country south of Dothan, and she had him out on a blanket with her. She went back into the garage for clothespins and didn't see the pack of dogs that had been roaming in the woods out there for a couple of weeks. I had shot at them a few days before and killed one, but they kept coming back. They came in over the fence and she didn't see or hear them until they had him and were taking him back over the fence. We didn't find him for eight months and this was all there was. The bones had been picked clean, and they came apart when we tried to carry him out."

"Jesus Christ," Bobby said. "What about your wife?"

"She blamed herself, of course," Wilkes said, "and so did I for a long time, but it hasn't helped. She was in the hospital a long time after, and now we live apart."

"It's terrible," Bobby said. "I've never heard anything like it. I don't know how you survive something like that. When Jim died, we just pretended the war had done it, and that somehow made it better, but he was a grown man. That's a lot different."

"We didn't survive it," Wilkes said. "We lived, but we didn't survive. We buried him like this, in pieces, on our family plot in Alabama, and then I went away for a year because I hated her for what had happened. But all I thought about was him in pieces, so I came back and dug him up and brought him here to put back together. It seemed like the only thing I could do."

Bobby looked at the gentle young man with the bones in his hands and cried. Wilkes was crying quietly too, looking out the back door at the Gulf. "It won't bring him back," Bobby said.

"Yes, it will," Wilkes said. "As much as I can have."

At noon Mother Sauls, Bobby, and Junior took Linda into Tallahassee for her checkup with the doctor and to get Mother Sauls her typewriter. Mother drove, and Bobby sat in the back with Junior. After a time on the road he told them about Wilkes's son. Linda cried, and Mother got angry at Bobby for upsetting her with the horrible details of the dogs dragging the baby off. They rode in silence for a time while the pines whipped by and the clouds grew thick overhead, and when Linda spoke, she was calm and there was great compassion in her voice.

"Poor man," she said. "I wish there was something we could do. It seems like such a strange and wonderful thing he's doing."

"We can leave him alone," said Mother Sauls. "He's doing what he has to do. It's all he has left."

"He thinks it will bring him back somehow, doesn't he?" Junior said.

"No," Bobby answered. "He knows he can't do that. It's something else, something a long way from that. He's just putting it back together, that's all."

"I still want to do something," Linda said. "Maybe I'll bake him a cake."

They dropped Mother Sauls and Linda off at the doctor's office near the hospital, and then Junior drove. Bobby had him head across town to some secondhand shops where they might find a typewriter. He had not been there in many years, and the town had changed a great deal, but he found the street with the stores he was looking for with no difficulty and then had Junior turn off where he remembered the icehouse had been.

The squat, faded wooden building was still there but a green-and-white sign said it contained a bicycle repair shop now. Bobby told Junior to stop in front, and he got out of the car and walked around to the side of the building where the loading platform had been. The platform was there, in the shade of two big oaks Bobby did not remember, cluttered now with bicycles, and behind them the huge, sliding wooden doors with cast-iron rollers and fittings leading to the interior where the ice machines and blocks of ice had been. A young man with long hair tied back in a ponytail was kneeling beside a bicycle up on a stand, working on the gears with a screwdriver and wrench. He looked up and smiled as Bobby approached.

"Yes, sir, can I help you?" the young man said cheerfully.

"This used to be an icehouse, didn't it?" Bobby asked.

"A long time ago," the young man said. "There's been a bunch of things in here since then."

"I'll bet," Bobby said, looking around. "I used to run ice out of here down along the coast."

"Really?" The young man set down his tools, wiped his hands on the denim apron he was wearing, and stood above Bobby on the platform. "When was that?"

"In the thirties. It was a long time ago."

"I'll say. I guess that was pretty interesting, wasn't it?"

"I didn't do it long," Bobby said. "I went back in the oyster boats after that. I just wanted to come by and see the place. I have a lot of memories about it." He finished and felt embarrassed for telling too much. But the young man was polite, and if he wasn't really interested, at least he faked it beautifully.

"Sure," the young man said. "Come back anytime. I'd like to hear about it. I've never run into anybody who was an iceman." He picked up his tools and started back on the bike.

"I just wanted to see it this once," Bobby replied. "Thanks." He stood on his tiptoes to look into the darkened interior, but all he could see was bicycles. Nothing about the place but the platform was the same. He didn't know what he wanted to find, anyway, but it was good to see and feel the same wood on the platform. He ran his hand over the wood, slick and dark in places from so much wear. The young man looked up again and smiled, and Bobby quickly withdrew his hand.

When Bobby got back to the car, Junior was bouncing impatiently in the seat. "What was that all about?" he asked.

"This used to be an icehouse," Bobby said. "I used to deliver ice from here."

"Jeez, Granddad," Junior exclaimed, "I didn't know about that."

"Nobody does," Bobby said.

They found a likely-looking secondhand store on Gaines Street, a few blocks from the icehouse, and both went in to look for a typewriter. The interior was filled with old furniture and table after table of every describable kind of junk, and it smelled like the middle pages of an old book. A fat man wearing shorts and a shirt open to the navel approached Bobby, with his hands clasped together in front of his voluminous stomach.

"Yes sir," the man exclaimed. "Looking or buying?"

"Maybe both," Bobby said, instantly disliking the man. "We're looking for a typewriter."

"Let me show you what we've got," the fat man said. He turned about and waved for them to follow. Junior peeled off at a table with a pile of ancient fishing tackle, but Bobby kept close behind the man, who led him into another, darker room in the back of the store. Though somewhat less cluttered, it gave off the same smell of old things. There was a row of beat-up file cabinets, some office furniture, and a table with two rows of typewriters.

"Electric or manual," the man said with a flourishing turn toward Bobby.

"Manual, I think," Bobby said. "It's for my wife. We don't need anything fancy." He thought that sounded funny, and he was glad Mother wasn't there to hear it, but he said nothing to correct it. He had talked too much at the icehouse and didn't want to do it again here.

"Got a great little Olympia here," the fat man said. "Thirty-five dollars."

"Let me try it," Bobby said.

"There's paper in it. Have a go."

Bobby stepped to the machine the man had indicated and tried the carriage return, then typed: "Bobby Sauls, Sauls Cottages, Gulf of Mexico."

"Great little machine, isn't it, pop? And you look like you could be a finger faster than most folks with that extra one there. That must come in pretty handy."

Bobby stuck the little finger into his right nostril, showing the rest as if a normal hand suspended there. "It'll do," he said. "And I'll take the typewriter."

The fat man lifted the machine from the table with a loud, sweating grunt, and Bobby followed him to the front of the store. Junior was browsing along a table containing old trophies of every size and description. There were bowling and golf trophies, each with a little figure engaged in that activity on top; baseball and track trophies, most engraved with a particular person's name and event. Bobby stopped in front of a trophy about a foot tall, with the figure on top frozen forever in midstride, holding up a garland of olive leaves. There was a brass plate on the base, but it contained no inscription. He picked it up and turned it slowly in his hands.

"I'm going to get this for Wilkes," Bobby told Junior.

"Why?"

"I just want to," Bobby replied. "That's all."

Linda was elated; and Mother Sauls looked drained, but she perked up and became quite animated when Bobby and Junior picked them up at the doctor's office and presented her with the typewriter.

"It's perfect," she exclaimed. "I can't wait to get started with it. Thank you both for finding it."

They rearranged their seating once again, Bobby and Junior moving to the back. Mother Sauls uncharacteristically suggested they stop at a nearby drugstore for ice cream before starting back. Junior went into the store for the cones while a radiant Linda told Bobby about her visit. Bobby looked at her beautiful teeth and listened.

"The baby's dropped, Granddad. That means it'll only be a few days now, maybe even tomorrow. He said if this wasn't my first he'd have me stay in the hospital because it would probably come before we could get back up here. But I told him my wonderful family would get me here as soon as I start labor."

"You just be careful," Bobby said. "Don't do too much."

"I just wonder where your husband is during all this," said Mother Sauls. "What an asshole, running off like that."

"It's better that way," Bobby said, touching Linda's arm. "We'll take care of you."

"Men are such idiots," Mother said.

"I can't worry about that now," said Linda. "I'm going to concentrate on having this baby, and the rest will take care of itself." She ran her hand down Bobby's face, then kissed him on the cheek.

"I got something for Wilkes," Bobby said, pulling the trophy out from under the seat. "It can be from all of us." He showed it to them and expected Mother Sauls to blast him about it, but she didn't. She took the trophy from him and turned it around to look at it from all sides.

"It's a beautiful trophy," she said. "And a fine idea. You've done good, Bobby."

"I think so too," Linda said sweetly. "It's lovely."

"I'll give it to him when we get back," Bobby said proudly.

Junior came back with the ice cream cones and they started for home. When they had cleared the town and were passing through the pine woods again, Bobby could see the black bottoms of the clouds, low on the horizon at the end of the road, and then the sweeping, gray lines of the rain itself over the water when they crossed the bridge over Ochlockonee Bay. And a mile before they turned off the blacktop into the yard of the cottages, the first rain in more than two months was exploding on the windshield and drumming on the roof. When Mother Sauls pulled up in front of the store, they all were whooping and cheering. And there, in the middle of the yard between the cottages, was Psychic Ike, dancing through the delicious downpour wearing only his boxer shorts, with Wilkes laughing and applauding from the side. Ike saw the little party in the car and waved, and then he took off in a run toward the beach and attempted a hook slide. It turned into a long skid on his ample backside, with feet and arms high in the air, and ended up in a beautiful, two-revolution spin that he pretended, with a wave of his hands, was planned all along.

Junior bolted from the car and ran to join Ike in a bizarre, impromptu dance, while Bobby walked slowly down the yard in the cool, steady rain to present Wilkes with his trophy. He looked back toward the car and saw

Linda and Mother Sauls standing close together under an umbrella Mother kept in the car. They started out toward Linda's cottage, and she motioned him once with a back-handed toss of her hand to keep going. Bobby stopped a few feet from Wilkes, who was completely soaked and shivering, but still smiling.

"We have something for you," Bobby began. "For what you're doing. I guess we should wait for you to finish, but we can't." He held out the battered trophy to Wilkes, who looked at it a long moment, then took it and embraced Bobby.

"You people are really something," Wilkes said in Bobby's ear. "What a strange and wonderful place."

Bobby shook his hand, then started down the yard to his own porch to be with the rain. Ike and Junior were watching, their dancing suspended by the little ceremony, but they said nothing when Bobby passed.

He went to his chair on the porch and put his feet up on the milk crate. The Gulf was churning, and he could only see a short distance out on it because of the rain, which was straight up and down and white over the water. He was glad to have been wrong about the rain coming, but he wished he could have stayed at the cottages to smell it coming. The city was no place to be when it was raining on the Gulf, but then he remembered Wilkes and the trophy and was glad he had gone. He closed his eyes and listened to the rain on the roof and in the palmettos around the cottage and imagined the horrible scene of the dogs dragging away the baby. But then the image of Wilkes working patiently day after day on the skeleton bloomed over it, and Bobby quite suddenly and with great joy understood that it was Ike's prediction come true. He could feel their lives being changed by what Wilkes was doing, though he did not understand why. It was simply enough for now to have them all pulling together for something, for Wilkes and the skeleton, and to have the rain—its simple, incessant droning a palpable gift of sound, a long time missing. And before he could get very far in examining Wilkes's place in the prediction, it wrapped and lulled both the cottage and Bobby Sauls into a common, inseparable, and dreamless sleep.

When he woke, Bobby was in the kitchen of the cottage where he'd found the flying fish, the aftermath of Jim's suicide, and the exquisite sunlit bedroom of the woman on the ice route. He came up from sleep in a gradual, fluid way, already in motion, and at first believed he had gotten up from his own chair to get a beer. Following through on that gauzy thought, he even opened the refrigerator in the darkened cottage. His confusion on finding it empty jolted him fully awake and spun him around for a look at his surroundings. The kitchen was empty. It was not his, but he could not remember how he had gotten there. He scratched his head with his extra little finger and felt his wet hair, then looked out the back porch. It was still raining, and he could see his own cottage near the beach in the cloud-formed early dusk and Mother Sauls's bulky form in the light from their kitchen window. He did not remember walking over at all, and he thought for a moment he had fallen asleep on this porch. But then he remembered his chair and the milk crate and the sound of the rain in the palmettos.

Afraid but bolstered by the lingering memory of the

new strength he had felt in discovering Wilkes's link to the prediction, Bobby went through the kitchen and into the living room. He stood a long time in the arched opening between the rooms and gazed with quiet astonishment on what he found. All four walls of the room were completely covered with seashells in all the varieties he had ever seen. He touched the wall nearest him. They were real: scallops and coquina, conch and oyster. Even in the dull light that rendered them all the same dusky tan, they were very beautiful. He went around the perimeter of the room, dragging his hand over the shells in an up-and-down wavelike motion. Every inch of wall was covered, with no two shells of the same species adjacent to each other. Where shells of odd shapes abutted, coquinas filled the resulting gaps, creating an extraordinary mosaic. Bobby stayed with the shell walls and filled his eyes and mind much longer than he had any of the other visions, because he knew that they, like the others, would be gone when he came again. And he would come again. Whatever was happening in the cottage was as much a part of this mystifying summer as the heat, and the people, and now the wonderful rain. And if this and all the rest were nothing more than the pathetic ragings, beautiful and sad, of his disintegrating mind, the world perhaps was a more astonishing place than he believed.

THIRTEEN

No one had seen Ronnie since his raving beaching of the boat. Junior came back from a trip to Carrabelle the day after they took Linda to Tallahassee with word that none of the oyster fleet knew of his whereabouts either. One of the men said he thought Ronnie had taken a job in a sawmill in the area near Port St. Joe, but he wasn't sure. Junior was the real worrier of the family, and he showed it at supper with Mother Sauls and Bobby, while the second afternoon rain in as many days pounded in the yard and spilled in sheets from the roof into the palmettos around the cottage. Bobby was trying to work out a formula regarding the relative merits of predictable, afternoon showers versus other regular events, like bowel movements, and he had nearly decided that rain, because of the mood it created, took precedence, but Junior would not shut up about Ronnie.

"He was pretty worked up the last time we saw him, you know," Junior said. "You didn't see it, Grandma, but he was a mess. I just hope he's all right."

"You sound like an old woman," Bobby said, looking out at the rain. "You're too young to be worrying like that." The rain was gusting against the cottage in sheets, accompanied by frequent lightning flashes and the great, round tumbling of thunder that carried so well over the water. Bobby wanted it to last all night because it was so good to sleep with, especially the thunder as it grew more and more distant. But this was not that kind of rain.

"Well, I *am* an old woman," said Mother Sauls. "And I think somebody ought to find him. His wife's about to have a baby."

"He'll show up," Bobby murmured to the window. "He always does."

"What if he's gone and drowned?" said Junior. "He wasn't doing too well when he left in that boat, you know."

"We'd have heard," said Bobby. "Leave it alone."

"Maybe the sharks got him," Junior said. "We'd never know then."

Bobby brought his gaze back inside and glared at Junior. They finished the meal in silence, and while Mother Sauls put on a pot of coffee, Bobby asked her about the typewriter.

"It's great," she answered. "I'm slow, but at least I can read what I'm writing now."

"How far along are you?"

"My wedding," she said. "I'm writing about my wedding."

"Our wedding," Bobby corrected. "We did that together, remember?" Mother Sauls did not acknowledge him.

"Hey, can we read it?" Junior asked.

"No. I don't want anybody to read it," she said. "Bobby

knows all about it anyway. Get him to tell you, if he can remember."

Junior turned enthusiastically to Bobby. "What about it, Granddad?" he said. "Where'd you get married?"

"Jesus Christ, Junior," Bobby said. "You *are* an old woman. Why don't you go chase girls, or something?"

"There aren't any." Junior smirked. "Not around here."

"Then go off with one of those magazines and make something up. That's what you ought to be doing. We've got some on the rack up in the store."

"Don't start, Bobby," Mother Sauls said, rubbing Junior's head vigorously. "Junior's a good, sensitive boy. Don't you get him off in the wrong direction."

"Shit," Bobby said. "My knees hurt like hell."

Junior laughed like a terrier. Mother had just put the coffee out on the table when they heard Linda's yell. It was long and loud and came in over the sound of the rain like a siren, but Bobby could not make out what she was saying or if it was just a noise.

"That's it, I bet," said Mother Sauls. "Let's get going. Bobby, you go tell Ike and Mr. Wilkes and get the car going. Junior and I'll get Linda."

"What's going on?" Junior whined.

"It's baby time, fool," Bobby snapped. "Go help your grandma."

Mother Sauls was already crossing the yard to Linda's cottage, and Junior swung in tow a short distance behind. "Whoa, Grandma," Bobby heard Linda call. He went out in the rain, now suddenly irritating, and knocked first on Wilkes's front screen. Bobby could see Wilkes reading a book under the bare bulb in the living room. He got up and brought the book with him to the door.

"We're taking Linda in to the hospital," Bobby said. "I just wanted to tell you where we'd be."

"I heard her." Wilkes smiled. "So, this is finally it, huh?"

"Yes, I hope so. See you later."

Bobby left and hurried to Ike's cottage. He could hear the shower running when he passed the bathroom window so he stopped there, pressed his nose against the screen and called, "Ike, we're taking Linda in. She's started. Can you hear me?"

Ike's wet, bearded head appeared in a moment at the bathroom window, looming suddenly and not quite fully formed out of the steam. "What?" he said.

"Linda's started," Bobby said. "We're taking her in. They're coming now."

Ike looked over Bobby's shoulder out across the yard. Linda was being held along by Junior and Mother Sauls under a huge red umbrella that had Gilbey's Gin printed on it in white letters. Junior was carrying her suitcase in one hand and fighting to hold the umbrella against the wind and rain with the other, while trying to keep its canopy over all of them. Linda seemed to be walking easily at first, but then she stopped suddenly and grabbed her belly as a contraction hit.

"I'll get dressed and follow you up on the bike," Ike said.

"No, you don't have to do that," said Bobby.

"I'm coming," Ike said. "Get going."

The others had nearly caught up with him, so Bobby hurried to get the car ready as Mother Sauls had asked. He started the engine, then got out and opened the back door for Linda and Mother.

"Can you drive?" Mother Sauls said sternly. "This is very important."

"Yes," Bobby replied.

"Don't shit me, Bobby." She was placing Linda in the back seat.

"I'm not, goddammit. I can do it."

"Go fast, but careful," she said. "Maybe you ought to let Junior drive. I want to be with Linda."

"I'm fine," Bobby said. "I'll do fine. Let's go."

He drove the car out onto the blacktop and quickly got it up to seventy. In a few minutes they were crossing the bridge over the bay. It was still raining hard, and the road was very black and slick-looking. The lights made beautiful, crazy patterns that crystallized and came apart in the water on the road and windshield. Bobby was concentrating as hard as he could, and he felt as though he might fly apart as well. But he gripped the wheel with both hands and held the car between the white lines with his clenched teeth.

When they had to slow down to go through Panacea, Bobby patted Junior on the shoulder. "Get me a cigarette and light it, will you, pal? There should be some up there on the dash."

Junior felt for the pack and found it over near Bobby's side, in front of the steering wheel. He shook one out, lit it, and stuck it between Bobby's lips. Bobby inhaled the smoke deeply and felt his neck and shoulders relax a little. He had not driven at night in fifteen years.

"How's she doing?" Bobby asked into the rearview mirror.

"Fine," replied Mother Sauls. "They're about five minutes apart. She's got a long time yet, but don't dawdle."

"It seems like you were in labor for days," Bobby said.

"Oh, my God," Linda groaned.

"Shut up and drive, old man," commanded Mother Sauls.

Bobby drove and did quite well for not being able to see the road half the time and having to recall himself from mixing with the fragmenting light reflections—until they had passed through Crawfordville and were on the last open stretch of road before Tallahassee. Bobby was asking Junior to light him another cigarette and didn't see the car a quarter mile ahead slow to begin turning off the highway onto a dirt road leading into the woods. He was watching Junior light the cigarette, and when he looked up they were closing in fast on the turning car. Bobby slammed on the brakes, and the car went into a slide, the back end coming around until they were sideways, heading down the middle of the road toward the other car. In the midst of the screaming from the back seat and his own confusion and panic, Bobby somehow remembered that you were supposed to steer in the direction of the skid, but Junior had already jerked the wheel from his hands to do that, and the car straightened just as they shot past the dirt road, barely missing the tail end of the other car.

They came to a stop on the side of the road, and Bobby rested his head against the steering wheel. He could feel his heart leaping in his chest and fought to keep from passing out.

"Is everyone all right?" said Mother Sauls. "Bobby, are you all right?"

"I'm all right," Bobby said. "What about Linda."

"I'm OK, I think," Linda said. "Just scared to death."

The driver of the other car came running up to Bobby's

window. "You folks hurt?" he asked. "I signaled a long way before I turned."

"I know," Bobby said. "It was my fault. We have a woman here who's going to have a baby. We have to get going. I'm sorry." He opened the door and got out slowly. He was very shaky and almost went down on the wet pavement, but the other driver caught him and leaned him up against the car.

"You'd better see a doctor, buddy," the man said.

"No, I just want to get to the other side," Bobby said. "Junior, you'd better drive."

He leaned against the man, who took him around the back of the car and helped him in. Junior slid over and took the wheel. "Thank you," said Bobby. "We have to go now. I'm very sorry."

"All right," said the man. "Drive slow, now."

Junior started the car, took it up to fifty-five, and held it there. Bobby laid his head back against the seat and closed his eyes. He had nearly killed them all. He formed a picture of what might have happened if Junior hadn't straightened the car—the rolls and flips and then the crash into the trees off the road. There would probably have been a fire too. A chill passed through him, thinking of Linda and the baby dying that way, and then he heard her cry out from the back seat.

"Oh, God, Grandma," she screamed. "I'm not going to make it. It's coming."

There was movement in the back seat, and then Mother Sauls's strong, calm voice came up over Linda's cries.

"Pull over where you can, Junior," she said. "Get way off the road. She's going to have it now, and we've got to give her more room."

"Now?" Bobby said, turning to look over the seat.

"Now. You scared her so bad, she's going to have it now."

Junior found a wide space of flat grass on the shoulder and pulled off. He got out and ran frantically out into the road, stood there helplessly for a moment, and came back to the car. Bobby was helping Mother get Linda into the front seat, with her legs out the open door away from the road.

"Watch for a policeman or something," Mother Sauls told Junior. "We're going to need some help."

"Someone's coming now," Junior said. "I see a light coming fast down the road."

Bobby looked up and saw the motorcycle coming at high speed. He saw by the shape of the rider that it was Ike and then Ike saw the car. He came up from his crouch over the handlebars and started braking and brought the Harley bouncing in behind the car. He set the bike on its stand and ran up to Bobby.

"What happened?" he said.

"She's having the baby," Bobby said. "We're not going to make it to the hospital."

"Goddamn," said Ike. "Linda, you all right, honey?"

"It's crowning," said Mother Sauls. "I can see its head."

Ike pushed Bobby gently aside and went on his hands and knees. He took off his riding gloves and handed them up to Bobby.

"I can help," he said. "I delivered a shitload of gook babies in Vietnam."

"Good," said Mother Sauls. "Because it's been a long time for me."

Ike stood again and took Bobby by the shoulders. "Get together all the rags you can find," he said. "The cleaner the better. Tear up your shirt if you have to, and then go around and support her from the other side. You'll have to hold her up when she pushes. We'll get it from this end."

Bobby went out to the road and got the keys from Junior and opened the trunk, but there was nothing he could use. He took off his soaked shirt and told Junior to do the same and took them to Ike.

"We need a flashlight," Ike said. "The light in here isn't enough."

"There's one in the glove compartment," said Mother Sauls. "I hope the batteries are still good."

Ike found the light and shined it between Linda's raised, open legs. Bobby saw the bulge against her pelvic floor and the spot of hair that was the baby's head, and then it drew back.

"I think it's coming down OK," Ike said. "Get around behind her now, Bobby. Let's try pushing."

Bobby went back around to the other door and crawled in behind Linda. He lifted her by the shoulders and helped her place one hand on the dash and the other on the top of the seat back. "All right, baby," Ike said. "You push, and Mother, you massage it down from the top."

Bobby could feel the strain in Linda's back and shoulders and her gasping for breath as she pushed, but she did not cry out until Ike told her to ease off and she fell back into Bobby's arms.

"I can't do it," Linda said, sobbing.

"Yes, you can," Ike said soothingly. "You have to. Now rest, and when you feel another contraction coming, sit up and push. It'll only take a few more. I saw more of her head that time."

"Her?" said Bobby. "Is it a girl?"

"I don't know yet," Ike said. "I've just always thought it was going to be a girl, a beautiful girl, like her mama."

"Oh, shit," cried Linda. "Here we go." She struggled to sit, and Bobby pushed from behind.

"Push, Linda, push," said Mother Sauls. "It's coming. Come on, girl, push."

"Almost," Ike said. "You help more from above next time, Mother. We've almost got the little sucker." He was holding the flashlight in his armpit and was wiping his hands on Bobby's shirt as he watched Linda's pelvis. Bobby thought he had never seen a greater look of concentration on a person's face.

"Here comes somebody," Junior shouted from the road. "I'll flag them down."

Bobby watched a pickup truck roll to a stop before Junior's waving arms. Junior hopped to the driver's side and in a few moments was running back to the car.

"He's got a CB, and he's radioing for an ambulance. He said he'd stay around until it came in case we need any help."

"Great," Ike said. "We're all right now. Come on, Linda. One more time."

Bobby pushed her up, and she strained with a mighty, sustained yell.

"Good," Ike exclaimed. "I've got the head. Keep going so I can get the shoulders and pull her out."

"Ahhhh," Linda screamed.

"I've got her," Ike said. "She's almost free. It's a girl, Linda. It's a girl!"

Bobby looked over Linda's shoulder and saw Ike pulling the baby's legs from her mother. She came out very
slowly, with Ike pulling, and then there was a gush of
fluid and she came quickly then, and Ike had her all and
was holding her upside down by the tiny ankles. He cradled her in one huge arm and wiped some of the gauzy
film from her face and head, and then he placed his mouth
over her mouth and nose, sucked out, and spit some fluid,
and the baby cried.

"Hooray," Bobby shouted.

"Help her deliver the placenta," Ike said to Mother Sauls.
"And then start packing with the rags. Bobby, you
tear off a strip from this one so I can tie off the cord.
Just let her lie down now. We have to be careful of bleeding."

Bobby gently let Linda's head come down to the seat.
She was panting and whimpering, but she grabbed his
hand and squeezed it. "My baby, my baby," she said.

"She's fine," Bobby said. "You'll have her in just a minute." In the distance he could hear the whine of the ambulance siren. He went around the car to Ike and tore a
long strip from one of the shirts. Ike took it and tied off
the cord a foot from the baby. Bobby sat down hard in
the wet grass. The rain had stopped. Down the road he
could see the flashing lights of the ambulance. Everything
was going to be all right.

The man from the truck came up and handed Ike a
towel. "Here," he said. "Maybe this will help."

Ike cleaned the baby with a piece of the shirt, then
wrapped it in the towel and laid it on Linda's abdomen.
"Here you go," he said. "Start mothering."

Bobby was still sitting in the grass hugging his knees,
and Ike sat down heavily beside him. The woods were

dripping behind them, and the crickets and frogs had started up again. "I just remembered," Bobby said. "It's funny how it doesn't seem important anymore, but what about the finger?"

"She's got it," Ike said.

Linda was taken to the hospital, and the family followed and slept downstairs in the lobby for a few hours, until they were sure both mother and baby were fine. Then in the morning they all trooped back down to the coast and spent most of the day in bed. Bobby sat on the porch and thought about Wilkes and the skeleton and the prediction, and he decided Wilkes may actually have come there to resurrect his son, but that was too much for even Bobby to accept, though it would have caused quite a stir, and he rejected the notion. It had nothing to do with the Gulf, anyway, and he knew the Gulf had to be in it somehow. When he could reach no firm understanding of where Wilkes and the bones fit in, he slept in the chair. At two o'clock Mother Sauls fixed everyone a huge lunch, and then she and Bobby went back to the hospital, with Mother driving, to see the baby.

They found Ronnie standing before the big glass windows of the nursery when they got there. He was unshaven and sagged in the shoulders, but he seemed very happy, and hugged Mother and Bobby while he pointed out the baby.

"There she is," he said. "A six-finger Sauls, just like I told you. Ain't she beautiful?"

"Yes, she is," Bobby said. "Did you hear what happened?"

"Yes," Ronnie said soberly. "Junior called and found

me at the sawmill this morning. I'm working there now, you know, and old Junior, he watches out for me. I'm sorry it happened that way, but I'm thankful they're both all right."

Bobby wanted to tell him that Ike had done it, but he didn't want to start that all over again, now that the baby had been born with the finger.

"If you'd been around, it probably wouldn't have happened that way," Mother Sauls said.

"I know," Ronnie said. "I'm sorry. I'll make it up to her somehow."

"Have you seen her?"

"No. She won't let me. I tried, but they told me she wouldn't see me."

"I don't blame her," said Mother Sauls. "But she'll probably come around. You're the baby's father, after all."

"Yes," Ronnie said, smiling. "I am. Ain't that great?"

"Well, we're going in to see Linda," Bobby said. "Why don't you wait and come home with us?"

"I can't go back with you," Ronnie said. "Not until she takes me back, but maybe we could go out and celebrate a little. This is a pretty big thing, you know. A man should celebrate the birth of his first child."

"Not me," said Mother Sauls, starting down the hallway to the rooms. "You two lunatics go if you want to, but I'm visiting with Linda a bit and then going home."

"How about it, Bobby?" Ronnie said. "Let's go have a few to celebrate. I heard about a great place out on the Parkway we can try."

"All right," Bobby said. "You'll have to drop me at the cottages, though."

"Fine. I'll wait for you in the lobby. Tell Linda I love her."

The place Ronnie took Bobby to celebrate was called Studebaker's, a former all-you-can-eat cafeteria converted into a beer and dance hall specializing in fifties rock 'n' roll and containing a full-sized Studebaker convertible pointed at the dance floor. They got there about eight o'clock. It was a Thursday, and the crowd was still thin. But the music had started, and the DJ was standing on a platform and lip-synching the song with great enthusiasm. There was a little fence with a space on the top to place drinks running around the perimeter of the oval-shaped dance floor, and there were tables on a raised level around that. Ronnie led Bobby to a table near the dance floor and a waitress in an orange-and-white cheerleader uniform approached the table.

"They thought of everything here," Ronnie said. "Even cheerleaders. Isn't that great?"

"It's wonderful," Bobby said lamely. "But the music's too damn loud. Let's get out of here and go to a bar."

"Just a few minutes," Ronnie said. "Let's give it a chance. I've heard some great things about this place."

"What are you guys having?" asked the cheerleader.

"Two Buds," Ronnie said. "Thanks, sweetie."

When she left to get their order, Ronnie watched her little swaying pleats all the way to the bar. "She's cute as shit, ain't she, Bobby?" he said.

"Let's just drink the beer and get out of here," Bobby said. "This place is for kids. They're all goddamn college kids." He took out a Camel and lit it. The Studebaker was full and pointed at the dance floor, and the kids were cruising.

A couple appeared next to them at the table, and the young man assumed a stern face. "Excuse me," he said. "This is our table."

"I didn't see anything on it," Ronnie said.

"We went out to dance," the boy said. "And we want this table back."

"Get another one," Ronnie said. "We're here now."

Bobby looked at the girl. She was very young and very beautiful, but it was a distant, superior kind of beauty. He knew she would keep quiet and remain a step removed from the confrontation, but her boyfriend would know how to get the table back for her. There was no backing down in her young, aggressive face, and Bobby suspected she demanded the same in her suitors.

"This is the table we want," the boy said. "It's ours." He was taller than Ronnie, well built, and seemingly in good shape, but there was no chance he could handle Ronnie in a fight, especially since Ronnie's last one had been a defeat at the hands of Ike. He would be wanting to prove to himself he still had it, and this kid would be the one to pay. Bobby didn't want to see it. He looked at the muscles tighten in Ronnie's jaw.

"Come on, Ronnie," he said. "We're going anyway. Give them their table."

"It's not their table," Ronnie said firmly and without emotion. "If he wants it, maybe he'd better try moving me off it."

"You're not worth it, you dumb hick," the kid said, and if he had let it go at that he might have walked away, but he added, for the girl, Bobby thought: "Redneck faggots."

Ronnie jumped out of his chair, grabbed the kid by the shirt at the throat and hit him once with his right hand square on the forehead. The kid went limp, the girl started screaming, and Ronnie let him settle to the floor. Some kind of fat security guard made the mistake of grabbing Ronnie's shoulder from behind, and Ronnie decked him too, and then the guy made a second mistake and got up so Ronnie could hit him again. Then the guy drew his gun and Bobby got scared, but Ronnie stopped when he saw it and put up his hands.

"You got the drop on me, sheriff," he said. "I'll go quietly."

They held Ronnie in the office of the place while they waited for the police, and he and Bobby smoked and said nothing. The security guard sat on top of the desk and swung his foot out and back, banging against the desk each time, and occasionally rubbed his jaw where Ronnie had hit him, but he said nothing either.

Bobby's head was swimming from all the activity of the past twenty-four hours. Now Ronnie was going to be arrested, and he would have to figure out a way to get home. That bothered him more than anything; that, and what a fool Mother Sauls would say he was for going with Ronnie in the first place. On top of that, they had never gotten the beers they ordered.

"Sir," Bobby said to the security man. "Can I have a beer? I'm thirsty as shit. That's all I came in here for."

"No way," the man said. "You're drinking's over for the night."

"It never started," Bobby said. "But that's beside the point now." Ike was probably at home now, drinking up all his beer and looking at the Gulf. Bobby hoped he wasn't going to get hauled in too.

"I didn't hit anybody, you know," he said.

"I know," said the security man. "I know who did the hitting."

There was a knock on the door, and two uniformed policemen were let in. When Ronnie saw them he bolted and tried to squeeze between them and out the door, but they caught him and pinned his hands behind him. "What about the old man?" one of the cops said. Ronnie was still struggling to get away. The other cop had pulled out his card and was reading Ronnie his rights.

"No," said the security guard. "He just came in with Buster there. He's harmless."

They hauled Ronnie away, kicking, and Bobby didn't get a chance to say good-bye. He was afraid he might never see Ronnie again, and so he felt bad about not saying something. He looked around the strange office with the perfect lighting and furniture and felt the pounding of the last two days. He had nearly killed them all in the car, and he would never drive again. The cottages on the Gulf seemed very far away for the first time in his life, and then, as he always did when things started closing in, he remembered the woman on the ice route. But it was like someone else's memory. None of it was real anymore, but nothing had replaced it. Bobby hoped the prediction would come true soon, and he would know it when he saw it, because the only thing he could honestly say he felt was the great, hollow emptiness of the distance between him and Mother Sauls, the huge squatting ghost of fifty years. He closed his eyes and pictured Wilkes at work on the tiny skeleton and the yellow room he worked in, but it meant nothing. He couldn't make it mean anything.

"You can go now," said the security man.

Bobby looked at him a long time before comprehending what he had said. "Can I use your phone?" he finally said. "My ride just left."

FOURTEEN

Bobby was walking up from the beach, where he had positively identified a dead Portuguese man-of-war he had watched floating in on the tide after supper, when he saw Mother Sauls and the black man coming slowly down the yard toward the water. He didn't recognize the man at first, but as they got closer he was pleased to see that it was Cleveland, whom he and Dink Maynard had run into on their way out to Crowder's Sink the night they had gotten so drunk. He hurried up the yard and met them halfway.

"Hey, Cleveland," Bobby said. "I'm glad to see you. Did you run out of wine again?"

Cleveland looked at him but did not smile or say anything. He turned to Mother Sauls, who looked somber and withdrawn.

"What's wrong?" Bobby said.

"Cleveland has some bad news about Dink, Bobby. He came to tell you himself."

"He's dead, isn't he?" Bobby said.

"Yes," said Cleveland. "I just found out about it myself, Bobby. He died this afternoon. They found him out on the highway not far from here, up by the Episcopal camp. He wasn't hit or nothing. They said he died of heatstroke. They say his truck was somewheres up the road. Nobody knows why he was walking or where he was headed."

Bobby looked at the ground. The grass was coming in very well with all the rain. St. Augustine was a very hardy grass and could stand almost anything. It always came back. "He was my best friend," Bobby said. "All my life."

"I know," Cleveland said. "That's why I came to tell you."

Bobby looked up into the man's kind face. "Thanks for telling me, Cleveland," he said. "I'm glad I found out from you. There aren't too many of us left now, are there?"

"No, sir. There ain't many left at all, Bobby. I'm sorry. I'll be going now. It's a bitch, ain't it."

"It's a bitch," Bobby said. He stood there in the yard and watched Mother Sauls and Cleveland go back up the yard to the store, and then he noticed that it had become nearly dark while they talked. He remembered a game he had played when he was a boy, where he would watch the sky as night came in, then look away at something on the ground for a moment, then look back at the sky and note the changes. You couldn't see the night come in if you watched only the sky, because it was stealthy. But the minute you looked away, it would change. You could never see it happen. He didn't see it now, because he was thinking about Dink, but he knew it was hanging around out there, ready to come down when he wasn't looking.

Bobby put his hands in the pockets of his khaki shorts

and stood there in the yard until it was dark and for some time after. Mother Sauls passed him on her way back to the cottage from the store, but she didn't stop or say anything, and Bobby didn't really see her. He turned when she was gone and looked at the black Gulf, and then he made his way back to the cottage too, climbed up on the porch, and sat in his chair with his feet up on the milk crate. He could see the lights of a shrimper working its way out into the Gulf against the black night that seemed so thick and unyielding. And then Junior came up out of the darkness from the beach, carrying his surf rod and a small stringer of whiting, which he brought up onto the porch.

"Pretty good," Bobby said. "Were they biting good?"

"For about a half hour," Junior said. "I lost a bunch of them, and then they just quit."

"Clean them outside," Bobby said. "You know what Mother will say if you get scales all over the kitchen."

Junior nodded and started back out the screen door to the cleaning table they had set up at the side of the house.

"Wait a minute," Bobby said. "I'll get the light and come out too." He got up from his chair and went into the unlit kitchen, where the outside light switch was mounted. He felt for the switch above the sink, flicked it on, and turned to get a beer from the refrigerator when he bumped into Mother Sauls. He hadn't seen her sitting at the table.

"Jesus, I'm sorry," he said. "What the hell are you doing here in the dark?"

"Thinking about Dink," said Mother Sauls.

Bobby got his beer but couldn't think of anything to

say to her, so he stood in the dark holding the cold can for a minute, and then he gave up and went outside.

Junior was at the cleaning table under the bare bulb that was screwed into a socket fixed to the side of the house, cleaning and filleting the whiting. A large group of moths was already circling the bulb. Bobby watched Junior expertly fillet the fish, wash them, and place them in a pile at one side of the table. He remembered the beer and drank some. The night pressed in from the palmettos and pines that grew very near the house on that side, and the air smelled like wet newspapers, but Bobby was absorbed in watching Junior's long, skinny hands.

"You've got piano player's hands," he said. "I just noticed that."

"Fishy hands." Junior laughed. "Sometimes I can't get the smell out for days." The moths were circling his bulb-lit yellow hair.

"We should get a piano and give you music lessons. Mother would like that too. I'll tell her about it."

Junior said nothing and started work on the last fish, the biggest, which he had saved for last. Bobby finished the beer and tossed the can into the garbage pail with the fish parts.

"A friend of mine died today," he said.

Junior stopped working on the fish and looked at him. "Who?"

"Dink Maynard," Bobby said. "You remember. He was over about two weeks ago, and we went out. That big fellow without any teeth."

"I remember," said Junior. "He seemed to be having a lot of fun."

"He always had fun. I knew him all my life, and he

always had fun. I hadn't seen him in a long time, but when I did, it was just like before."

"Was he old?"

"No, he was my age. We grew up together."

"I'm sorry," Junior said. "I guess you'll miss him."

"You don't expect your friends to die," Bobby said. "Family, yes, but not your friends. It's too much like accepting you're going to die yourself, because your friends are tied to you in another way. It's like you've made them up out of yourself. But your family's not like that. Does that make any sense?"

"Sort of," Junior said. He finished the last fish and put it in the pile with the others, and Bobby heard the crickets in the trees and palmettos.

"I've got to put these in the freezer," Junior said. "Are you coming?"

"I think I'll take a walk," Bobby said.

"I'll get the light," said Junior. "I'm sorry about your friend."

Junior went inside with the fish, and Bobby watched the moths until the light went out. Then he went around the cottage and up the long yard to the road. He stood in front of Ike's huge palm sign with the big letters on it that said Psychic. He lit a cigarette and then started walking up the road to see if he could find the place Cleveland had said Dink Maynard had been found.

There were no cars, so Bobby walked in the middle of the road, straddling the intermittent white line. He heard the crickets in the palmettos on both sides of the road, and once he looked up and saw the Milky Way, like a long, thin cloud of smoke. Cleveland had said they found Dink down the road from the Episcopal camp. That was about a mile from the cottages. Maybe he had been trying to get there. If his truck had conked out anywhere on this stretch of road, that was where he would have come, to get Bobby to help him. Together they could fix anything. When they were teenagers they rebuilt a 1932 Ford coupe and drove the hell out of it on the coast roads. There were hardly any people down here then. It was isolated and wild, the streams and ponds full of bass, and the woods home to a good many black bear. After the war people from Tallahassee started building vacation houses, and everything changed.

Bobby walked and remembered riding at night in the coupe with his head out the window in the wind, the cool rush of air and the way it smelled. In the distance he could see the lights on tall poles at the Episcopal camp. It must have been somewhere along here.

Bobby left the middle of the road and crossed to the sandy shoulder. Dink would have been walking on the right side, the side toward the Gulf. After the sand there was a thick buffer of palmettos and then the string of beach houses. Bobby walked along in the sand, looking, *feeling* for a sign of Dink. Thank God they had gotten back together, he thought. It would have been bad for Dink to have gone out with that old business between them.

He stopped and gazed into the still palmettos. This was the place. He could feel it. This was where old Dink crossed over. Bobby remembered when his father died. They'd had an old-fashioned wake and laid him out on two big planks between sawhorses in the living room, where they'd found him the day before, slumped in his chair. Bobby had sat and looked at the old man on the table for two hours, and then he'd said good-bye. Dink should be here now. It was hard to say a proper good-bye to somebody who wasn't there. Bobby wished he'd been with Dink. If he couldn't have saved him, at least he could have shook his hand and said good-bye.

FIFTEEN

When Linda brought the baby home from the hospital, they moved into Psychic Ike's cottage, next to the big palm sign up near the road. All that first, clear, humid morning Ike carried things from Linda's place to his. Around noon, when the clouds for the now-regular afternoon thunderstorm moved in, Linda brought the baby out, dressed in her tiny diapers and a pink bonnet. She supervised the last few trips, and then the three of them went down to the beach to show the baby the Gulf for the first time.

Bobby watched them from his chair on the porch while Mother Sauls pounded her typewriter in the living room. The baby took one feeble glance at the Gulf and then buried her face against Linda's breast and wailed. Ike threw his head back and laughed. They looked like they had been a family all along. It made Bobby feel strange to look at them, and he got up to get a beer so he wouldn't have to see any more. It had all happened so fast, though he believed it had been happening all along, as Ronnie suspected, and Bobby didn't know how he was supposed to feel.

"Did you know about that?" he asked Mother Sauls at her desk.

"About what?"

"Linda moving in with Ike."

"Yes, she told me at the hospital she was going to do it."

"Well, I like Ike and all," Bobby said. "But I expected it would end up this way if the baby was born *without* the finger, not with it."

"It doesn't matter," said Mother Sauls. "I think they're in love. They have been a long time. But who knows. You know how Linda can be. When she was in high school she went for anything in pants."

"It just seems strange," Bobby said. "What are they going to call it? The baby, I mean."

"Rosebud."

"What? What kind of a name is Rosebud?"

"A rather beautiful name, I think," said Mother Sauls. "It was your great-aunt's name."

"That's right," Bobby said, lighting a cigarette. "I'd forgotten. But it's still a silly name, and this is all pretty goddamn confusing. Is she going to marry him?"

"I don't think they've thought that far," said Mother Sauls. "Besides, she's still married to Ronnie, in case you've forgotten."

"I haven't forgotten," he said. "I'm not senile."

Bobby went into the kitchen and got his beer. He looked out the window at Ike, Linda, and Rosebud on the beach. There was a good wind off the water blowing Ike and Linda's hair back, and they were facing out to sea like two people in a photograph he had seen once in *Life* magazine. Even the clouds above the water were the same, and then he remembered the photograph had been in black and white, just like the scene they were in. The thunderstorm was coming early today. Bobby looked at the clouds and wondered how Ronnie was getting along in jail. Linda had showed no emotion when he told her about it. She just slightly shook her head and smoothed the baby's thin patch of hair. Bobby took the beer into the living room and watched Mother type for nearly a half hour.

"At least it was born with the finger," he said at last. "I'm going to see Wilkes."

"I'm glad you're here," Wilkes said, as he put the skeleton away in its box and the pillowcase with the few remaining bones back under the coffee table.

"I didn't mean to interrupt," Bobby said. "I'll just be quiet and watch if you want to keep working."

"No, I'm done for the day. In fact, I'm almost finished with it." He completed his housekeeping and sat back on the sofa. Bobby took the rocker facing him.

"I'm glad you're here," Wilkes continued, "because I don't like thunderstorms. I've always been a little afraid of them and I see another one's coming."

"You're kidding," said Bobby.

"No, always have been. I like to have someone around. It's good to talk when there's a storm outside."

"I look forward to them," Bobby said. "It's the best thing about living here. Sometimes there's quite a show out there on the water. You can see everything."

Wilkes shook his head slowly from side to side. "I'd

rather not," he said. "When I was a little boy, a lightning bolt hit our house, and I saw a ball of fire in the kitchen. I've been terrified ever since."

"I didn't think you were afraid of anything," Bobby said. "I just had that feeling about you."

"I'm afraid of many things," Wilkes replied. He turned his face toward the window. The rain was beginning gently, in advance of the real storm. The light in the room had gradually grown dim and gray since Bobby came in. Wilkes looked out the window a long time, then turned back and showed Bobby his casual, distant smile.

"Tell me," he said. "How long have you and Mrs. Sauls been married?"

Bobby looked quickly around the room, as if to find the answer somewhere on the walls. "I don't know," he said. "Fifty-some-odd years. We don't celebrate anniversaries."

"Do you still love her?"

"How the hell do I know? We're old. We don't think about stuff like that. What a question."

"I'm sorry," Wilkes said. "I didn't mean to embarrass you, but I thought since you'd been together so long you could tell me. My folks were always openly affectionate and close, but my father died pretty early, and they weren't married as long as you. I just wondered what it's like to be with the same woman so long."

"You just get used to it," Bobby said. "That's all."

"I wonder. I haven't spoken to my wife in more than six months," Wilkes said.

"You have different circumstances, I would think."

"Yes," Wilkes said. "I don't suppose I'll find out what it's like to be married fifty years."

Bobby shuffled his tennis shoes under the chair and looked at them. The rain was coming harder in the yard. Ike was the only one that knew, the only one he had told in fifty years. Even Linda, Ronnie, and Junior had no idea. They thought his was just an old marriage, subject to the same distances familiarity brings in any old relationship—and maybe even closer than most. He and Mother Sauls went everywhere together; she still laid out his clean clothes every morning, cooked, mended, and cared for him. Only Ike had seen something inverted, and that was because of his own peculiar, ultramasculine bias. But even Ike knew little of the great, silent squatting ghost between them: invisible, familiar, and even benevolent, but always with the potential to turn mean at any moment. Bobby lit a cigarette and blew the smoke up and out through his nose, packing the bitter, filterless tip occasionally with his tongue. He wondered for the first time in his life why he had never considered throwing in the towel. He could not believe that sometime in the early days of their reconstructed relationship, or at any of a thousand points along the way, he had not determined to chuck it all and strike out on his own, but he had not. He had bent to the task of being Mother Sauls's husband, and in the face of Wilkes's questions and his confession to Ike, he did not know why. Listening to the rain and then the thunder in the gray, interminable comfort of Wilkes's living room he tried for a time to figure it out, but it was like trying to find something lost in a dream. And the rain, instead of being the soothing companion of deliverance, was becoming as much an irritant as the heat had been.

"I would guess the death of your son pulled you two even closer," Wilkes said.

"It's hard to say," Bobby replied. "We expected it to happen. He had a hard time in the war and never got over it."

"I suppose your wife took it very hard."

"Yes," Bobby answered, but he did not really know how she had taken it. They had never talked about Jim. Bobby looked at the box containing the baby's bones. Someone had had to do a great deal of work to get Jim's body ready for the funeral, and they had hired a painter to do the room over, but Mother had taken the sheets and the throw rug and burned them in a fifty-five-gallon drum in the yard between the cottages. That was all Bobby knew about how she felt.

"Are you a religious man?" Bobby asked Wilkes.

"No," Wilkes said. "Not particularly. Certainly not anymore."

"I was thinking you might be planning a resurrection," Bobby said. "With putting the skeleton together and everything. It would be wonderful if you could. I've never really bought that whole thing, you know, but if I saw it here, I might."

"I don't know," Wilkes said.

Bobby looked out the window at the lightly falling rain. The bark of the pines in the yard was black and slick, and he could see the luminescent green fronds of the palmettos around Linda and Ronnie's place jumping when the drops hit them.

"Well, I've got to be going," Bobby said. "It doesn't look like it's going to be much of a storm. I've got to talk to Mother about some things."

"I'm fine," Wilkes said. "I see there's been a change in some of the living arrangements." He walked Bobby to the door and held open the screen. The rain was coming gently and steadily, and the electrical storm was some distance to the west.

"You mean Linda and Ike? Yes, I don't know how that's going to work out yet, but they seem happy."

"I should go see the baby, I guess," said Wilkes.

"If you can," Bobby said. "Good-bye."

He went out into the rain and headed for his own cottage. Ike was coming from Linda's place with one more box, covered with a plastic garbage bag.

"Hey," Ike said. "Rosebud smiled at me. She actually smiled."

"It was gas," Bobby said. "Everybody knows that."

He made it up onto his porch and shook the rain off his baseball cap and then lit a cigarette. Mother Sauls was still working at the typewriter. Bobby stood on the porch and watched her through the doorway. She held her head very high and looked down through the bottoms of her bifocals at the page she was working on. Then she looked out the window a moment at the rain, or something much farther back, and returned to the page. Bobby approached her and placed a hand on her shoulder.

"I want to talk to you," he said. "You have to stop for a few minutes."

Mother Sauls turned in the chair to look at him. "More visions?"

"No," Bobby said firmly. "It's about Jim. Come over here so I can see you. Let's sit on the sofa."

"I don't want to talk about Jim," she said. "I want to finish what I'm doing."

Bobby took her hand and pulled her from the chair. "You must," he said. "Please. It's important."

She followed reluctantly, like a child being led to punishment, and allowed herself to be placed on the sofa. Bobby pulled up his reading chair and sat a few feet away. When he reached in to find his voice again, it was rough, deep, and distant.

"Tell me how you felt about Jim," Bobby said.

Mother Sauls looked at him with alarm in her eyes. "Why?" she said. "What are you talking about?"

"I want to hear how you felt about him, how you felt when he died. When I came back down to the beach after being in his cottage, what did you feel? And after that— the weeks and months and years after he did it. I really don't know, you see. I don't know at all."

"He was my son," she said, as if to end it.

"He was my son too," Bobby exclaimed. "And I felt like something was cutting me up inside with hot razor blades, but you wouldn't let me tell you that, and you never said anything about him."

"Why are you doing this now?" she said. "Why after all this time?"

Bobby felt himself dangling dangerously close to the root of it all, and it was like a rush of cool air. It made him strong, but he backed off at the last second, as he had been trained to do for fifty years. He could not confront her with that yet. "Because it's all right for you to ignore me," he said. "But not Jim. You can't ignore Jim and pretend it didn't happen. He can't be punished for what he did, don't you see? He can't be punished by you or anybody else."

Mother Sauls struggled to get up from the sofa. "That's not it at all. You don't know anything about it," she said. "Not a damn thing."

"Then tell me," Bobby pleaded. "Tell me. The rest is unimportant, but tell me about Jim."

"I can't," she said, and stood up and left the room.

Bobby remained in the swirling residue of their tension and watched the lessening rain in the yard. He tried to conjure up the normally calming image of the woman on the ice route, an image he had fought to repress for so many years so that he might slide away on its smooth sheets and waving brown grass, the winding strength of the veins on her hands, and the painful mockery of the extra finger she adored. But when he needed it, it was not there. In its place was the somber, monochromatic image of Mother Sauls hanging clothes on a line in a wind from the Gulf, changing from a young to an old woman with thoughts he did not share, sinking deeper into a silence to which he now believed there was no end.

Bobby got to his feet and shook the kinks from his painful knees. The thunderstorm had been reduced to a dripping from the eaves, and he went out into the yard by way of the front door so he would not pass by Mother Sauls at her typewriter. Wilkes was back working on the skeleton, and there was laughter from Ike and Linda's place when he went by. Bobby walked west in the coquina at the edge of the blacktop until he grew tired, and then he sat down with his back against a neighbor's mailbox post and looked at the road. In a few minutes some kids in a convertible, probably on their way back to Tallahassee, slowed and stopped opposite him. Bobby was unaware of them at first, but he looked up when one of them called to him.

"Hey, old-timer," the kid said. "You all right?"

Bobby nodded.

"You want a beer?"

"Sure," Bobby said. "I could use a beer."

The kid got out of the convertible, and the others laughed. He brought the beer to the side of the road and handed it down to Bobby.

"Don't stay out too long, pop," the kid said softly. "And watch for cars."

"Thanks," Bobby said. He could not tell from the kid's words and tone whether he was being teased or not, but he didn't care.

The kid got back in the car, and they were off again. Bobby watched them until they were out of sight, and then he opened the beer and drank it with his back against the mailbox post while he chipped with his fingers in the coquina.

SIXTEEN

Ike and Linda brought Rosebud over for a visit with her great-grandparents on Saturday afternoon. Mother Sauls fixed a big pitcher of lemonade and served it on the porch in the middle of another thunderstorm that came up unexpectedly and with great force out of the west. One minute the Gulf was shining like a sheet of polished, blue aluminum, and the next it was a dark slate color and churning under fast-moving clouds and lightning. The downpour lasted only a few minutes, but the overcast and rough water of the Gulf stayed on, delaying the sailing expedition Junior had planned for the afternoon. Bobby held Rosebud on his lap and watched Junior pacing impatiently along the screen.

"This is just great," Junior complained. "When's this thing going to clear out of here?"

"It will," Bobby said. "They always do. Just give it a few more minutes. It's still pretty rough out there for sailing, Junior."

"The lightning's stopped," Junior said. "Can't I go out? I can handle it in this kind of sea, and there's a good wind."

"I know," Bobby said. "Just give it a little while longer." He held Rosebud up to look at her face. He thought she looked exactly like Ronnie but didn't say so. She had the same wide face, deep-set eyes, and flat nose, but that could have been said about any of the Sauls. She decidedly did not look like Ike, but then, nobody really knew what Ike looked like under all that hair. Maybe Ike thought the baby was his, and the extra finger had been thrown in to keep everybody happy, or maybe the legacy of the finger was only in the water they drank, but it didn't matter. She was there, and Ike was her daddy now. The baby cried, and Bobby took her down and held her across his shoulder.

"Better take this diaper," Linda said. "She'll spit up all over you."

Bobby took the offered diaper and placed it between his shoulder and the baby's face. "I know all about babies," he said. "I remember when you were just this size."

"I don't know shit about babies," said Ike. "This one scares the hell out of me."

"Bullshit." Linda laughed. "You ought to see the big lug with her. He's a natural. He coos and pets her and damn near cries himself to sleep every night, he's so happy."

"I don't get any sleep," Ike said. "Not anymore."

"You'll all have to quit cussing that way," said Mother Sauls, "or she'll grow up talking like a sailor too."

"Can't I go out now, Granddad?" Junior said. "It's all gone."

Bobby looked at the Gulf and then the sky. They were

both nearly the same uniform gray, separated only by the thin, bluish line of the horizon. There was still the occasional distant rumble of thunder behind them on the mainland, but he could see the sky growing lighter out over the Gulf. "All right," he said. "But stay in front here, and don't go out too far."

Junior dashed off the porch and ran to get the dinghy and sail from the tin lean-to on the side of the house. Bobby handed Rosebud back to Linda and lit a cigarette. Mother Sauls was drinking lemonade and looking at the water; except for the comment about their language, she was apparently uninterested in their conversations. In a couple of minutes Junior appeared again, dragging the dinghy behind him down the narrow path through the palmettos on his way to the beach. He got it to the sand and lifted the aluminum mast into its slot behind the middle seat, and then he started unfurling the sail. There was still a great deal of wind, and Junior had some difficulty with the sail. But he stayed with it. Beyond him the water was a dark gray, relatively calm close in, but churning out beyond the sandbar. Bobby thought it was a little silly to be going out while it was still rough, but he knew Junior was a good sailor and would stay where they could see him.

Junior hooked the boom with the loosened sail to the mast, and then, while Bobby was watching and with no warning, a spear of lightning he would later swear was pure blue shot from the clouds and struck the aluminum mast with a horrendous crack, instantly setting Junior's hair on fire and knocking him to the sand.

Linda screamed at the sound, and Bobby jumped to his feet. Ike was already through the screen door and charging down to the beach. Bobby knew Junior was dead, but he did not think about that. He followed Ike to the beach as fast as he could. Ike was over Junior feeling for a pulse in his throat. Junior's eyes were opened and burned, and his hair, eyebrows, and lashes had been burned off. Bobby momentarily caught the sickening smell of burned flesh passing in the wind. Ike bent over and started mouth-to-mouth resuscitation, and Bobby picked up one limp hand out of the sand and held it. In a moment Linda and Mother Sauls had joined them. Bobby could hear Linda sobbing and the baby crying, but Mother Sauls was quiet. She went around Junior's body so she was facing Bobby and dropped to her knees in the sand, and then a long, low moan started coming from her throat.

"Is he breathing?" Linda cried hysterically. She was holding the baby tight against her with both arms. "Did you check for a pulse?"

"He doesn't have one," Bobby said. "He's dead."

"You don't know," Linda said. "He can't be. Ike can save him." She leaned over Ike's back, holding the baby in her right arm and supporting herself with the left. "Bring him back, Ike," she said, almost as a whisper.

"He's dead," Bobby said. "I saw it happen. Nobody could live through that."

Ike moved his hands to Junior's chest and started massaging, then back to his mouth for two more breaths. He kept that up for fifteen minutes, but each time he stopped to listen and feel, there was no response from Junior. Ike finally sat back on his heels with one great, hairy hand on Junior's chest.

"Better call the sheriff," he said. "He's dead."

Mother Sauls's moan grew into a wail. She covered her

face with her hands and fell face first into the sand. "Not Junior," she cried. "Oh, not you too, Junior." Bobby did not try to comfort her. He put his arm around Linda, who stood looking down at Junior in pure disbelief, and then he went back to the cottage and into Junior's bedroom and took a blanket down from the closet to cover him. It had happened so fast, they had never heard the thunder. Bobby remembered the old people saying if you heard the thunder, you were all right. He hoped Junior had not felt anything.

It was very difficult to move and impossible to think, but Bobby made his way from Junior's bedroom out to the porch and looked at the scene on the beach. It was unreal; he could feel nothing yet. They were all still out there, and Mother Sauls was still prone in the sand. Bobby took the blanket down to the beach and pulled it out full over Junior. Someone had closed his eyes for him. It bothered Bobby to be putting a wool blanket over Junior in the steamy humidity after the storm, but he tried to be rational and told himself it did not matter anymore. Still, it was something he knew he would remember with some revulsion for the rest of his life. He stood for a long moment looking at the inert form of the blanket in the sand, and then he let himself feel the sadness. It was like his body was one long, hollow, hot pipe. The clouds of the storm were breaking up and moving away, and above them was a perfectly blue sky.

Bobby went to Mother Sauls and lifted her shoulders from the sand. He brushed the sand from the backs of her hands and helped her stand. "Come inside, Mother," he said. "It's over."

"My baby," Mother Sauls said.

Ike appeared to be the only thing holding Linda up. She still had no expression and was not crying. She held the baby close and allowed herself to be led away from Junior by Ike.

"I'll call the sheriff from the store," Ike said. "I want to get Linda and the baby put down first."

"Thanks," Bobby said. "I guess there's really no hurry, is there?" He sounded to himself as if he were trying to be very strong and take control, but it was not the way he was feeling. He took Mother Sauls's arm and urged her up the path to the cottage. Wilkes was standing in the yard, but he turned abruptly and went back to his cottage before they got to him. The sun had come out, and there was no sign of the storm at all overhead, only the thin, wispy, trailing edge of a gray cloud disappearing to the east. Bobby could feel the heat coming up in waves from the wet grass. He took Mother Sauls into their bedroom and helped her lie on her back. He got a wad of tissues and placed them in her hand, but she did not use them. The tears ran down her face and onto the pillow, and she let them go. She was staring up at the ceiling, but Bobby knew that look and knew she was seeing something else, and poor, silly, fragile Junior was gone.

"Can I get you anything, Mother?"

She shook her head, and the tears came harder. "What chance did he have?" she said. "It was always against him."

"He didn't suffer," Bobby said, hoping that was true. He sat on the bed beside her for a few minutes, holding her hand and remembering the awful sound of the lightning hitting the mast. He took the tissues and wiped her face. "If you're all right, I've got to talk to the sheriff when he gets here."

"Go," said Mother Sauls. "I'm all right."

Bobby went out to the porch and then into the yard. He could see Junior's form under the brown blanket on the beach. While he was standing there a sheriff's car pulled up at the store, followed by an ambulance. Bobby started up the yard to meet them. Ike came out of his cottage, met the deputy, and brought him down to Bobby. They shook hands without speaking, and Bobby led the way down to the beach.

The deputy pulled back the blanket and examined Junior. "How long ago did this happen?" he said. He pulled a shiny black notebook from his pocket and started writing.

"About a half hour ago, I guess, maybe a little longer," Ike said. "Wouldn't you say, Bobby?"

"Yes, that's about right. Look, can we get in the shade to talk about this? I'm not feeling too good."

"Certainly, sir," said the deputy. "I just need a few things from you, and then I'll have the deceased removed."

"Thanks," Bobby said. "We can go up to my porch."

They went back to the cottage through the steaming grass and took their places on the porch, Bobby and Ike facing the Gulf, and the deputy with his back to it. Bobby had a clear view of Junior's blanket-covered body, and he watched it the whole time the deputy questioned them.

"How did it happen?" the man asked. "Did he go out in the storm?"

"No," Ike said. "It was after the storm had passed. It was still windy, but it had stopped raining, and we all thought there would be no more lightning."

"There was only that one more," Bobby said. "He went down to the beach and was getting the boat ready to go out, when it hit the mast he had hold of."

"Did you see it?"

"Yes. I was watching him the whole time."

"How exactly did it happen?"

"The bolt—it was pure blue—hit the mast and passed through Junior. It was massive. There was a big crack when it hit, and Junior's hair caught on fire. Ike tried a long time to get him breathing again, but I knew it wouldn't work." Bobby hoped they would hurry and finish before the tide came in and rolled Junior away, or before someone came along and went poking under the blanket. He stared at the form on the beach, which now seemed so small, and then there was a twitching beneath the blanket where the feet would be. Bobby stood up and stifled a little cry with his hand when he saw Junior stagger to his feet and lurch drunkenly down the sand for thirty yards before crashing to his face in the surf, where he floated, arms out and unmoving, like a fallen bird.

"My God," Bobby cried. "Look, didn't you see that? He got up and ran down the beach. He got up!"

Ike stood and put both his big hands on Bobby's shoulders. He looked to where Bobby was pointing, and then he gently pressed Bobby back into his chair.

"No, Bobby," Ike said. "It doesn't happen that way."

Bobby rode in the back seat with Linda, Ike, and Rosebud, in the car following the hearse. He fixed his gaze on the black web of veil that lay on the neck of Mother Sauls, who rode in front. There were delicate strands connecting thicker, larger sections of the pattern, and Bobby was intrigued by its resemblance to an enlarged snowflake, a huge, black snowflake engulfing Mother Sauls's face and neck. From there it was easy to imagine black snowflakes descending on them all as they stepped from the car into the brilliant sunlight that seemed to burst in silent explosions between the oaks and pines of the cemetery. Bobby imagined huge, black snowflakes descending slower than parachutes, some getting hung up in the trees where they drooped in the branches but did not melt, others settling softly on the trimmed grass, the unreal green of the grass showing through in the pattern. He imagined the sound they would make as they collapsed in the grass and then their sound as they closed around ears and nose, shutting out the world. As he watched the men draw the long box containing Junior from the rear of the hearse, he realized with a clarity like sunlight what was now going to happen to Junior, realized that being stuck in the ground was worse than being struck by the lightning bolt. And in that moment, very near to running from the place himself, Bobby knew that was why he had seen Junior get up and run down the beach.

In the two days following Junior's death Bobby had rarely left the porch but remained with his eyes fixed on the horizon or scanning the changing water. Slowly, the events of Junior's death coalesced with the crazy pattern of the summer, but it gave him no comfort. If Junior had resurrected on the beach, it would have been the thing Bobby had been dreaming of since Psychic Ike's arrival and pronouncement—and long before even. But he had not resurrected. And if Bobby's vision of Junior getting to his feet and dashing down the beach was the manifestation of the prediction, there was no beauty in it, no lesson but hopelessness. In the silence of his meditation Bobby came to perceive Junior's death, as well as Wilkes's skeleton, the persistent but now imageless memories of the woman on the ice route, and even the miraculous happenings in the empty cottage, as unrelated, meaningless events in a world too combative to offer salvation. He was saddened and embarrassed to have only now discovered something everyone else already knew.

Bobby shook off the daydream about the black snowflakes and escorted Mother Sauls to the front row of folding chairs under the canopy before the open grave. They were burying Junior in the Sauls plot at Shiloh Church. Bobby could see the headstones of his mother and father and, a few feet away, those of Mother Sauls's parents and then Jim's. Bobby took his wife's hand and held it. Rosebud started crying, and Linda got up and carried her out among the graves. The minister stood before the little row of chairs and started speaking, but Bobby did not hear him. He was watching Linda pass between the rows of graves with the sunlight in the baby's spun-glass tuft of hair. And then, beyond the graves, in a thinned stand of pines before the real woods began, he saw Ronnie standing with his hands clasped in front and his head bowed.

That afternoon there was no thunderstorm, and Ike helped Bobby pull the sailing dinghy from the beach, where it had been since Junior's death, up to the road. They attached a For Sale sign and left it. Mother Sauls had said she could not stand to have it around. Bobby remembered she had said the same thing about Jim's shotgun, and after Jim's funeral he had taken it out with him in the boat and dropped it overboard three miles out in the Gulf. When they were finished with the boat, Ike asked Bobby in for a beer, but Bobby said no and went back to his own porch to look at the water. Mother Sauls was typing away in the living room, but after his second or third cigarette Bobby heard her stop. In a moment she was standing behind his chair. They remained that way a long time, watching the hard silver sunlight on the smooth water, and then she spoke.

"I felt responsible," she said. "And there was that thing between us, and I couldn't talk about it."

"Responsible for Junior?"

Mother Sauls came around Bobby's chair and pulled up one of the other porch chairs so she was facing him.

"No, for Jim," she said. "You asked me how I felt about Jim, and I'm trying to tell you. Junior was nobody's fault. It was a horrible accident that could have happened only to poor, simple Junior, but I felt what happened to Jim was my fault because of the thing that existed between you and me. I put it there, and all those years he was growing up he knew about it, felt it between us, and everywhere he turned there was that big nothing, that silence."

"We loved him," Bobby said weakly. "We showed him we loved him."

"But he had to live in that awful emptiness that was meant for you," said Mother Sauls. "And it got so big there was nothing else, and I didn't know any way out."

"I put it there if anybody did," Bobby said. "It was my doing."

Mother Sauls looked at him a long time. Her face was soft and fleshy, but her eyes were very clear and present. Bobby had not looked that deeply into her eyes in many years.

"What's happening?" she asked. "Is there anything left?"

"I don't know," Bobby answered, taking her hand. "We can try. Tell me about Jim."

She looked away, stood, and walked to the end of the porch and came back to sit again. "I don't know where to start," she said. "You know, I wished for a long time he'd been killed in Vietnam instead of the way it happened. I was sure the pain would have been much less. I could have stood it, anyway, like any other mother who'd lost a son over there. When he came back, I could tell it had already been done, but he came back walking and talking, and then he had to finish it himself. See Bobby, it wasn't like you think. It wasn't the war that did it to him like you've always thought. It was what he saw there, yes, but only how it added in to what he already knew. It was the stillness of his world, the stupid game we were playing, and when I knew that, after he was gone, it was like trying to scream in a nightmare when you open your mouth but you can't make a sound. I didn't have a voice, Bobby." She smiled, and the tears came up in her eyes. "I tried to scream, but nothing came out." Bobby leaned forward, took her face in his hands and kissed both her wet eyelids.

"I couldn't say anything," she said. "Don't you see? I was hurt so badly, and then it got to be all there was of us, the way we were, and I couldn't change. I've been hoping for many years you'd break through and say, *enough*, but you never did; and now Junior's gone too. Death makes everything so small, Bobby."

Bobby held her palm against his face and caressed her extra little finger. "Why are you able to talk now?" he said. "Why is it all coming out now?"

"Because I've been watching you die this summer," she said.

That night they made love like people half their age, but with a great, pervasive sense of sadness, and then while Mother Sauls slept, Bobby went to the cottage of the visions with a flashlight. There was nothing in the living room or on the walls, so he went into the bedroom. It was made up for guests, the way it should be. Everything was quite normal. Feeling a purging combination of relief and disappointment, Bobby went back into the living room and sat on the sofa. He shined the light slowly along the walls, recalling how beautiful the shells had been and how clean and strong the walls had made him feel when he touched them. He lit a cigarette and hunted on the end table for the ashtray he knew Mother Sauls had placed in every cottage. After a few moments of groping he found it, and in the bottom was the shell of a solitary blue coquina.

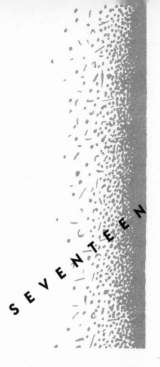

SEVENTEEN

Linda was on Ike's porch nursing Rosebud, and Ike had the Harley apart on the grass in the yellow evening, cleaning parts with his little paintbrush and jar of kerosene. Bobby sat nearby in a lawn chair drinking a beer with a can of bug spray between his knees. The rain had come late in the day, too late for the sun to steam everything up again, and the air was cool and soft and pleasant to sit in. Ike was in a talkative mood, and Bobby found it comfortable to listen and not have to think.

"We're thinking of moving on when the baby's old enough to travel," Ike said. "My old sugar mama, the one you and Junior helped me with, has decided she's dying of cancer, and she's moving in with a niece somewhere up in Georgia. It was good while it lasted, but there's just a few palm readings trickling in now, and it's really not enough to keep us going."

"What will you do?" Bobby said.

"Oh, get a job as a mechanic somewhere, maybe. Linda's never seen much other than this damn Gulf, you know. We were thinking of going to Atlanta or somewhere like that."

"Atlanta gets too cold, Ike. Don't go to Atlanta."

"Well, it's not settled yet," Ike said.

Bobby watched a dove light in the big pine tree next to Ike's disemboweled motorcycle. It cocked its minute head from one side to the other and then flew on to another tree. He remembered when he used to hunt them; he would bring home upwards of a dozen in an afternoon— they were very good roasted. Then he recalled the smell of those fall mornings when he hunted and the heart-stopping flutter of wings if he flushed a covey of quail or doves on the ground.

"I want to go somewhere too," Bobby said. "But I don't know where."

Ike did not answer. His belly completely obliterated his wide black leather belt and jiggled when he moved on his seat to another piece of the bike. Bobby watched him work and forgot what they had been talking about.

"I keep expecting Junior to come bouncing up," he said after some time.

"He was all right, " Ike said. "Goofy, but a good kid. I could have made a good mechanic out of him."

"How's Linda taking it?"

"As well as she can," Ike said.

"I wish I hadn't seen him get up like that," said Bobby. "It gave me hope for a moment." He heard the slap of a screen door and turned his head in the direction of the sound. Wilkes was coming across the yard toward them, moving through the thickening, faded color of the day with the somewhat sideways gait of a tired dog. But he smiled when he came up to Bobby.

"How about a beer, Mr. Wilkes?" Bobby said.

"No, thanks," Wilkes said. "I just had to come out and rest my eyes. How's the family, Ike?"

"Fat and noisy," Ike said.

"Ike and Linda are thinking of moving on soon," Bobby said.

"Nothing definite," Ike muttered. Wilkes sat down cross-legged in the grass and slapped at a mosquito. Bobby flipped him the can of spray, but Wilkes rolled it back to him and shook his head.

"How's it coming in there?" Bobby asked.

"Well, I'll be done tomorrow," answered Wilkes.

Ike stopped what he was doing and looked up.

"What then?"

"I don't know," Wilkes said. "I haven't thought about that."

"I'm sorry," Ike said. "About what happened to your boy. Bobby told me."

Wilkes looked at the grass and nodded. They all sat a long time without speaking in the heavy, fragrant air.

Bobby looked at the sky. It was streaked with long, high pink and purple clouds, and there was still a good deal of light in the sky above the cottages and over the Gulf, but it was dark in the grass under the trees where they were sitting. They were in the part of the day that was rolling under into night, and Bobby could almost feel the motion of it in his stomach when he looked at the sky.

"Bats," he said.

"Where?" said Ike.

"Everywhere. Look out there over the clear part of the

yard. You can see them against the sky. There must be twenty of them."

Ike looked and saw the small, erratically darting creatures in the clear part of the sky that rose like a thick column from the part of the yard where there were no trees.

"Those aren't bats," Ike insisted. "They're some kind of bird."

"No, they're bats, all right," Wilkes said. "You can tell by the shape of their wings when they glide. See there." One swooped low over their little gathering, and Bobby could just make out the serrated back edge of its wing. "You can tell by the noise they make too," he said.

"I'll be damned," said Ike. "What the hell are they doing?"

"Hunting mosquitoes," Bobby replied. "They're great for that. A few years back a guy down in the Keys built a tower and brought in thousands of bats to control the mosquito population down there, but when he let them go, they all flew off and never came back. I think there might even have been a million of them. They've always been around here in the summer."

"Far out," Ike exclaimed. "I want to see one up close. Can you catch them somehow?" He wiped his hands on a rag and stood up to look at the bats.

"I don't think so," Wilkes said. "They fly too crazy, and you wouldn't want to grab one anyway. They can be rabid."

"I'm going to catch one," Ike said. "Bobby, you got a ladder?"

"Over on the back side of the store," Bobby said. "What are you going to do?"

Ike marched across the yard to the back side of the

store, found the ladder on its side in the tall grass at the base of the building, and lugged it back to Bobby and Wilkes. Linda came out on the porch steps with the sleeping Rosebud and stood with the last light caught in her long, white skirt. "What's he doing now?" she said to Bobby.

"He's after bats," Bobby told her. "We made the mistake of showing him some, and now he wants to see one up close."

Ike placed the ladder up against his cottage. The top of it stuck a good six feet above the worn blue shingles of the roof.

"Give me your cap," he demanded of Bobby.

"You can't catch a bat in a cap, fool," Bobby said, but he took off the cap and handed it to Ike.

"I forgot something," Ike said, and he brushed past Linda and disappeared into the cottage. Linda came out into the yard and stood beside Bobby. Wilkes was still seated in the grass. Ike reappeared, putting on his thick leather riding gloves. "If he bites now," he said. "He'll get nothing but leather."

"He'd get that anyway," said Linda.

Ike perched Bobby's cap on the back of his massive head and started up the ladder. He scrambled out onto the steep pitch of the roof above the flat porch roof, went to the peak on all fours and stood straddling it.

"What now, King Kong," Linda called.

"I catch me a bat," Ike said.

He stood dark against the lighter sky like an animated gargoyle and started chittering in a high-pitched squeak. The bats were still darting everywhere about the trees and cottage.

"That's pretty good," Wilkes offered. "He's got talent."

Ike continued making his bat noises. He took off Bobby's cap and held it ready. A bat flew crazily over the roof but out of his range. Ike flexed his knees in a semi-crouch and waited. Another bat careened in close, and Ike shot out the cap. In the quickest movement Bobby had ever seen, he snared it in flight and brought it against his thick upper thigh. The cap jerked and hopped, but Ike held it firm against his leg. Then, with his other hand, he slowly balled the cap around the bat, held it against his chest, and scooted down to the ladder on his seat.

"Holy shit," Bobby said. "I saw it, and I still don't believe it."

"The man's got talent," Wilkes repeated. He was standing now, with his hands on his hips, shaking his head. "You can't catch a bat like that."

Ike came down the ladder, holding on with one hand and holding the cap-contained bat against his chest with the other. He reached ground and walked, smiling, to the others. They could see the thrashing of the animal under the cap. Ike stood before them with great suspense and ceremony, looking in turn from one to the other of them, and then, with a flourish of his free hand, he held out the cap. It was completely empty.

"Where'd it go?" Bobby stammered. "I saw you catch it."

"You thought you saw me catch it." Ike smiled. "A bat can't be caught that way. You ought to know that, old man."

"But it was moving under the cap," Linda said. "We all saw it."

Ike pulled the cap back against his chest, and with his

hand beneath, it fluttered from within again. "Yes, you did, didn't you?" he said.

Wilkes laughed and turned to go back to his cottage. "I've seen enough," he said. "I'm going to bed."

"Good night," Bobby said. "Let us know your plans, you know."

"I will," Wilkes said. "As soon as I know myself."

Bobby watched him all the way into his cottage. The Gulf beyond was flat and slick, as if a layer of urethane had been stroked on the surface.

"I've got to put Rosebud down." Linda sighed. "You're some trickster, big Ike. You really had us going, man." She shifted the baby to her other shoulder and started into the house. "Good night, Bobby," she said.

"Good night, darlin'." Bobby watched Ike get back down to work on the cycle, it was like a buffalo in a mudhole. Bobby could hear the crickets and cicadas in the trees, but the bats had gone. The real night had moved in when he wasn't watching, and he could feel it on his skin. He thought of the coquina he had found in the ashtray in the empty cottage and wondered how long it had been there. It had probably been part of some guest's shell collection, left behind because it was so small. But there had been coquina in the beautiful walls he had seen and felt, and the pure blue ones were very rare. A wall of blue coquina would be very beautiful, Bobby thought. It would catch the afternoon light and glow, and it would be like a sky of shells, a textured sky you could feel. It would be good to build a wall like that.

Ike was whistling a vague tune, and Bobby came back from the coquina to listen. In spite of his denials, there was something magical about Ike. Bobby watched his big hands move over the cycle parts, the hands that had so impressively captured a bat that was not there at all.

"Why did you do that thing with the bat?" Bobby asked.

Ike stopped whistling and looked at Bobby. "I thought we needed it," he said. "After the thing with Junior and all. And Wilkes. It's hard for me to be around him. It was getting too thick."

"You're right," Bobby replied. "It was quite beautiful too. How did you make it so real, though?"

"I'll tell you a secret." Ike smiled. "I had him up until the time you looked for him in the cap."

Mother Sauls was waiting on the porch when Bobby came home. She almost never sat on the porch unless there was company, but there she was when he came up the steps and through the screen door, sitting in a chair next to his, facing the water. All the lights in the house were out, but he could see her round, sad face in the triangular section of moonlight reflected off the Gulf. She motioned him with her eyes to join her.

Bobby sat and lit a cigarette. There was phosphorus in the thin line of surf again and a narrow path of moonlight angling out from the beach. When he closed his eyes, he could still see the phosphorus and moonlight. But he could only imagine the water.

"Wilkes says he'll finish the skeleton tomorrow," Bobby said.

"We'll have to do something," said Mother Sauls. "He's a very nice man."

Bobby closed his eyes again and took in the sharp salt air through his nostrils. It would take a long time, but it would be good to have the living room wall that faced the porch and Gulf covered with coquina. He could make it as beautiful as the walls in the empty cottage, only entirely of coquina. They could dig the lives ones from the sand and Mother Sauls could make chowder, and then he could build the wall slowly with the shells, the way he wanted it. There would be time. It seemed there was always a lot of time. He pictured the wall covered with the shimmering watery light from the Gulf in early afternoon, and then the flat, blue consistency of it in morning. When Mother Sauls finally spoke again, he was nearly asleep.

"Bobby, I want you to tell me about her," she said.

Bobby did not pretend he didn't know what she was talking about as he did with many other things. It was the first time she had ever asked. He opened his eyes and looked at the water and took a long time before answering. "What do you want to know?" he said.

"Everything," said Mother Sauls. "It's very important now. Did you love her?"

"Yes, I think so."

There was a long pause, and then Mother Sauls drew in a breath that Bobby could hear, and she began again. "Where did it happen?"

"I delivered ice to her. It was a little store down at St. Marks. Her husband was a fisherman."

"Did he know about it too?"

"No," Bobby answered. "I don't think so. I couldn't say if she ever told him."

"You're not telling me about her," said Mother Sauls. "I want to know. What was she like?"

Bobby closed his eyes and reached back for the image of the woman on the ice route, but her face was indistinct.

All he saw clearly was the view of the river from her window and the morning sunlight on her bedroom walls. "She was tall and dark, with wonderfully strong winding veins on the backs of her hands, and she laughed a lot a first," he said. "And she loved my extra finger. It was a long time ago, and I never saw her again after I quit the route and went back in the boats."

"Never?"

"There was one time, by accident, at a revival you and I went to, but we didn't even speak."

Mother Sauls sighed and looked at the water. Bobby stared at her profile in the vague moonlight. They had grown old together in spite of this thing between them that was somehow finally deflating like a bad tire—or they had grown old together because of it. He was still not sure which, and he did not know what would be left when it was gone. He was suddenly aware that it might have become the only glue existing between them, and a little panic started growing in his mind. But he thought about the bedroom by the river, and it went away.

"How long did it last?"

"About six months, I guess. That's all."

"That's all," echoed Mother Sauls sarcastically. "If you loved her, why didn't you go to her? She must have loved you too."

"She did. I guess I loved you more. I think I still do."

Mother Sauls uttered a small, bitter laugh. "Neither of us should be talking about love," she said. "I can't even stand to say it. We're not children anymore. I just want to know the way it happened."

"I've told you all I can remember. It was a long time ago."

"I know you've dreamed about her. I know you've sat

out here, hour after hour, year after year, thinking about it."

"Yes."

"I hoped at the time you would deny it," she said. "I hoped you would make up some story about that awful underwear that I could believe, but you didn't."

"I couldn't," Bobby said. "I was caught."

"It might have been different," said Mother Sauls. Bobby could hear the polished edge of anger in her voice.

"No," Bobby said. "It happened the way it had to happen."

Mother Sauls studied the water again for some time, and then she turned to face him. "So, who are we now?" she asked cuttingly. "Do you feel any different talking about it? Are you relieved?"

"No," said Bobby. "For some reason, no. It's like talking about somebody else's life. All along it's been like somebody else's life. It's far easier than I ever thought it would be, and that makes it mean nothing."

"You've always expected too much," she said.

"I wanted this to be different," Bobby said. "And it's not. It's like something the moths have eaten."

"I know this," Mother Sauls said softly. "She's not the young thing you remember. She's old like us, and maybe even dead. Have you made her grow old with you?"

"No," Bobby said. "I haven't. It doesn't work that way."

Bobby woke in the night with moonlight rolling up his bare legs and Mother Sauls snoring in the bed next to his. He reached for his cigarette pack on the nightstand and smoked in the dark on his back, blowing the smoke out into the channel of moonlight, where it found form momentarily before slipping out the window into the main night as a thin, accelerating stream. He felt the night inside him where the great silent ghost of his affair had been. She had finally killed and removed it, but the space was still there, and the night had been the first to find and fill it again. Bobby smoked and felt inside the things that had come in with the night. They were many, and they were not always pleasant. Bobby knew he would have to shrink the space or find something better than the night to fill it.

He got out of bed, put on his khaki shorts, and quietly went out to the porch. It was strange but the Gulf held no fascination. It was a still, smooth, ancient body of water. There would be no deliverance, no change in their lives because of the openness that had come too late. Bobby left the porch and went down the worn path through the palmettos to the beach. The hard-packed dry sand squeaked and sent up small flares of phosphorescence with each step. He lit a cigarette and stood looking at the water. He felt a confusing rush of ideas, emotions, and dreams flooding the space where the night had been. They filled his belly for a churning moment and then rushed upward through his body and spread out on the water with the smoke he blew at the moon—until he was truly empty. Then he flicked the cigarette from his hand and watched the high, end-over-end arc of its red ash all the way until it hit the water with a soft hiss.

He turned to start back toward the cottage and saw someone approaching on the beach, out of the darkness where the moon did not touch. It was a man wearing dungarees and a fishing cap with a long bill, and he was kicking up long sparkling flares of phosphorescent sand with each loping step. Even before he saw the smiling, toothless face, Bobby could tell by that distinct, wonderfully clownish walk, that it was Dink Maynard. He sat down in the sand right there and waited. Dink soon approached and sat down wearily and heavily next to Bobby as if he had just been out for a tiring walk down the beach instead of coming back from the dead. Bobby did not know coming back from the dead would be so tiring, and he wondered how long Dink had been walking and how he got there. He took out another cigarette, lit it, and handed it to Dink. Then he lit one for himself. He listened as Dink inhaled long and slow and then exhaled forcefully.

"Shit," Bobby finally said. "They told me you were dead. Old Cleveland himself came here and said you were dead. I mourned you for days and days, Dink."

"I was," Dink said. "But I didn't like it, so I came back."

"How'd you do that? That's not supposed to be possible."

"I just left and came back," Dink said. "It was easy."

"What was there about it you didn't like?" Bobby said. It was good to be sharing a smoke with Dink again, but he wished they had a bottle too. The night was long, black, and wide, and he felt he could stay out in the little breeze with Dink all night and not worry about anything.

Dink stretched out both legs in the white sand and crossed them at the ankles. He was wearing his old leather work boots with the rawhide laces. "I didn't like any of it," he said. "The food, the music, the stuff you have to do. And there wasn't any pussy—not even to look at. Everybody was real serious, so I left."

"That's good, Dink," Bobby said. "That's what I'd do too. It's better than that here, even at its worst."

"That's why I came back," Dink said, smiling. He still did not have any teeth.

Bobby thought a long time and decided he felt very good. "Tell me this, though," he said. "Is there really anybody in charge? Anybody running this whole thing?"

"There were rumors," Dink said. "But nobody seems to know for sure. It's a pretty good way to keep folks in line, though."

"Sure," Bobby said. He finished his smoke and lit another. Dink was still smoking his and was only halfway through it. Bobby looked up at the stars. "I had a dream once," he said. "I just remembered it, about the stars. I dreamed I could make out all the figures up there, the constellations, you know, that I had never really seen before. Oh, I'd made out the dippers, but not really anything else; but in this dream, I could see them all just as clearly as if you'd drawn a picture for me, and it made me happier than I'd even been. Just being able to make out those constellations made me the happiest man."

Dink was looking up at the stars too, and Bobby watched his friend's face in that minimal falling of light for what seemed like a very long time. And then Dink turned to him smiling and said, "The only thing is, I have to go back, you know."

"I knew that," Bobby said. "I'm glad you came, Dink."

They stood up at the same time and faced each other. "Well," Dink said. "I want to drop by and see old Cleveland before I go back."

"Sure," Bobby said. Dink stuck out his hand and Bobby

took it, then stepped closer and hugged his friend with both arms. When they broke apart, Dink was smiling his toothless smile.

"We shouldn't have let those ten years happen like that," Bobby said. "We've been friends a long time."

"It's all right now," Dink said. "I've forgotten all about it."

"Me too," Bobby said, "if you have. So long, old Dink."

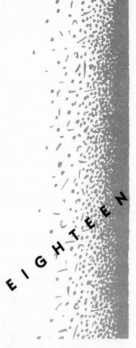

EIGHTEEN

The morning Wilkes completed the skeleton of his son was windy and overcast, but Psychic Ike set up the big striped umbrella in the yard between the cottages, and brought out chairs. While Mother and Bobby were having coffee, he came with Linda and the baby to say he was giving free palm readings. Bobby at first declined, saying the future was undoubtedly the same as the past, but Mother Sauls intervened with unusual good humor. She coaxed him into it on the grounds that the family didn't do enough together and told Ike they would be out after she got a little writing done.

While she worked, Bobby stalked about the house with his coffee and cigarettes, even more lethargic than normal for a morning. He stopped to look out each window at the low, blowing clouds that had transformed the August day into a scene reminiscent of a warm, late-winter day. He tried sitting in his chair on the porch, but it was no good. He could not find entry into the many protracted dreams and memories he had drifted with before. There was only the here and now, with its low clouds and incessant wind off the Gulf, billowing the screens and bending the palmettos along the path to the beach.

Mother Sauls left her typewriter and joined him on the porch. "Will it rain?" she asked.

"Later," said Bobby. "This is just junk blowing around now."

"I'm glad we talked yesterday," she said. "I know it hasn't changed anything, but I feel better."

"That's good," Bobby said.

"It's very strange after so long a time, but I was jealous when you told me about her."

"There's no reason," Bobby said. "It was over a long time ago."

"I was, just the same. I've imagined what she was like all these years, but hearing it from you made me jealous and angry as a young girl. I'm glad we talked about it, though, and it really is over now, isn't it."

"Yes," Bobby said. "Shall we go out and see what Ike can tell us about the next fifty years?"

Ike, Linda, and the baby were sitting in the lawn chairs under the umbrella. Bobby and Mother took their chairs and Ike enthusiastically slapped both palms on his grungy blue denims.

"Who's first?" he said.

"Has anybody seen Mr. Wilkes this morning?" asked Mother Sauls.

"No," Linda answered. "I wonder what he must be thinking. This has got to be a very strange day for him."

"He'll be all right," Ike said. "Let's get started. You go first, Bobby, Give me your hand."

Bobby put out his hand, palm down, toward Ike who flipped it over with a gentle twist and looked him in the eye. "We're coming on a bit testy this morning, aren't we, old man?" Ike said with a smile. "No matter. Let me look at this ugly leather."

"Go ahead," Bobby said. "Make up something pretty."

"The palm does not lie," Ike said. "Obviously, you have a very long life line—that's here. But this one, the one that runs completely off your hand, is your love line. It's very wide and deep too."

"If it's longer than his life line," Linda interjected, "does that mean he'll keep loving after death?"

"The relative lengths have nothing to do with each other directly," Ike said. "But since they're both so long, I'd say that was a possibility."

"Oh, Grandma, lucky you," Linda teased.

"Keep going," Bobby insisted.

"I see perseverance, intelligence, and loyalty. Very heavy on the loyalty. You'll have a good many more years of healthy life, as long as you don't quit smoking or drinking beer abruptly; and this little line that intersects both your love and life lines means you're connected in love to the same one person for life."

Ike lowered Bobby's hand and Bobby looked in his eyes again. They were gentle, distantly knowing black eyes, like many of the bigger fish have, and he remembered their trip on the water when they had seen the porpoises and what he had told Ike that day. Then it dawned on him what Ike was up to with the palm readings. He gripped Ike's hand firmly before letting go. "Thank you," he said. "Thank you for that."

"You're next, Mother." Ike grinned. "Hand it over."

Mother Sauls gave him her hand, and he rubbed the palm vigorously before examining it. Bobby watched the wind rippling the edges of the umbrella, and then he looked out and saw the rain coming in from the Gulf. It was still a long way out, but he could see it as a wide, gray swath curving from the clouds to the water, moving slowly toward land.

"And you, my dear," Ike was saying, "have the hands of an artist. This line is your creative life line, not to be confused with your regular life line. As you can see, it's deep and broad and intersects with your regular life line here. I'd be very proud of that. You, too, have a very long life line. It's not quite as long as Bobby's, but who's going to quibble over a few years, huh? I want you to see this, though. Look here. There's your love line intersecting your life line exactly like Bobby's. It's almost in the same place on the hand. You two were made for each other." He balled up her hand, kissed the knuckles, and handed it back to her.

"It's beginning to look that way," said Mother Sauls.

"Oh, jeez," Linda interrupted. "Here comes Mr. Wilkes."

Bobby turned and saw Wilkes coming across the yard from his cottage, carrying the box neatly under one arm. They all waited until he ducked under the umbrella, and then Bobby stood and offered his chair.

"No thanks, Bobby," Wilkes said. "But do you have a shovel?"

Bobby looked at him a moment, not comprehending, and then he understood and patted Wilkes on the shoulder. "I'll get it," he said.

Bobby left the umbrella and hurried to the back of the store, where the outdoor tools were kept. He found a shovel hanging on the wall and then went into the store and got a six-pack of beer from the cooler and carried both back out into the yard. A very light rain had begun to fall, but Bobby barely noticed it. He focused on the little group beneath the umbrella and thought about Wilkes's son being dragged off by the dogs, and Jim with the shotgun in his mouth, and Junior getting up to run away from death on the beach. And he stumbled, and the beer went flying. But he held on to the shovel and didn't go all the way to the ground. He used it as a crutch and pushed himself to a standing position before anyone from the umbrella could come to help. He waved them off and bent to pick up the beer cans by their plastic holder. And when he raised himself again, he was crying—because it was this burial they had been waiting for and not a yard full of flying fish or golden men in ancient wooden boats. And Jim was dead and Junior was dead and the woman on the ice route was dead or, worse yet, old as he was. And he had told Mother Sauls everything, and she had, in effect, forgiven him. And nothing had changed.

The rain was coming faster when he got under the umbrella, but it was a soft, simple rain with no lightning, and nobody said anything about it. Bobby handed the beer to Ike, and Linda held Rosebud tight against her chest, although there had never been any dogs around the cottages.

"I'd like to go down to the beach," Wilkes said.

"I'll carry the shovel for you," said Bobby.

They formed a little parade down the yard, with Wilkes in the lead. When they got to Bobby's cottage, Mother Sauls hurried in and got an umbrella for Linda and the baby while the rest waited. Then they all made their way down the path through the palmettos to the sand.

Wilkes put the box down, and they formed the best

circle they could around him with their few numbers. "I want to go very deep," Wilkes said, "so he won't be washed away."

"Of course," Bobby said. "It will be fine." He handed Wilkes the shovel and stepped back. Wilkes started digging. It was almost the same spot where Junior had been struck down. He dug easily in the soft top sand. Turning out big shovelfuls until he reached the hard-packed wet sand beneath, and the going was much slower. He dug another few minutes, widening the hole and squaring it off, and then Ike took the shovel and put his big back into it.

Bobby was standing so he could see Ike's face. It was straining with the work, and his wet, matted hair was falling down across his eyes, but his expression was one of deep concentration and benevolence, and Bobby realized he loved this man very much. He stepped forward and took hold of the shovel shaft.

"Can I put in a few licks?" he asked.

Ike looked first at Bobby and then up at Wilkes. "Of course," Wilkes said. "Why don't you finish it."

The hole was already about four feet deep. With great difficulty, Bobby took it down another foot, planing down the sides every few strokes so they were vertical. Then he squared it all off so it was a neat rectangle, got all the loose sand from the bottom, and stepped back. "That should do," he said.

"It's perfect," Wilkes said. "Thank you all." He looked around the little group of faces and then reached into the box and withdrew the tiny skeleton with both hands. Linda covered her mouth but she could not stifle a small cry, and Bobby looked and saw the tears coming heavily down Mother Sauls's face, but she made no sound.

Wilkes held the small skeleton and looked at it for a time, and then he got on his knees and carefully lowered it into the hole. He remained that way a long time while the rain came down on his back and shoulders, and when he stood up he was smiling.

"There," he said quietly. "It's done."

Bobby felt a great lightness steal through his body and with it the singular notion that more than Wilkes's skeleton was being buried there on the beach. He looked at Mother Sauls, who was staring blankly into the hole, and then at Linda, who clutched her baby and held out her hand to Psychic Ike—and it was as if they were all momentarily suspended at the apex of a giant roller coaster, just before hurtling down the other side to whatever lay there. Bobby felt in that moment he could see forever.

Wilkes took up the shovel again to begin filling the hole, and everyone moved, even if it was just to change the position of their feet. Then they heard the boat motor out in the rain and in a few seconds saw the boat itself break through, coming straight for the beach.

It was Ronnie, standing at the wheel of the same skiff he had come in the night he was drunk. Only this time it took Bobby longer to recognize him because of the rain and because he was wearing a coat and tie. Everyone on the beach stood still, frozen by the several incongruities of the moment, and then, fearing the worst and seeing there was no time to make it to the cottages, Bobby yelled to Ike to get in front of Linda and the baby. But Ike was already in a crouch and waiting. Linda ran to Mother Sauls, and they linked arms. The boat was still coming fast. Bobby would see Ronnie's expressionless face now, and the soaked white shirt sticking to his chest, but the strangest sight of all was the necktie flying off his shoulder like a pennant. He brought the boat in hard until he was twenty-five yards off shore, and then he cut the motor, sliced silently through the water the rest of the way, and plowed up on the sand, stopping a few feet from the hole they had dug for the skeleton. Wilkes slammed the shovel into the pile of sand from the hole and watched. Ronnie got out of the boat, looking first at Wilkes and the hole, and then he found the faces of Linda and the baby and smiled. He moved slowly and carefully away from the boat, and Ike came forward from the group and blocked his way. Ronnie looked up at Ike's face, and Bobby saw there was no meanness in his eyes this time.

"I didn't come to fight," he said firmly. "I came to see my wife and baby and to beg them to take me back." He turned away from Ike's hard-rock gaze and looked at Linda.

"I'm begging you, Linda, I can't stand it anymore, I've changed. I've got a good job at the new hardware store in Panacea now. I can take good care of you, and I want to come back." Ronnie stood with both hands out, palms up, but he did not try to go to Linda.

"You scare me," Linda said. "And I can't forget the things you called me. Everything's different now. I have a baby."

Ronnie took another step forward, and Ike had the good sense to step aside. He had said nothing since Ronnie's arrival.

Ronnie held up his right hand so Linda could see his extra little finger there. "You're my wife," he said. "We're blood, we're the same, you can't change that, Linda. It's not perfect—I can't promise you that, but it's real, and it's all we've got. I just want to talk, and hold my baby."

They stood looking at each other a long time in the rain, and then Ike slapped Ronnie playfully on the shoulder and shook him. "Look," Ike said, "let's all get out of this rain. Why don't you go continue this conversation inside. You three need to be alone, I think."

Ronnie looked long again at Ike and then at Linda. "Can we talk?" he asked.

Linda handed Rosebud to Mother Sauls without a word and started back to the cottages. Ronnie hurriedly squeezed some of the water from his jacket and tie and followed her up through the palmettos, smoothing back his wet hair. Bobby watched until they were in their cottage and the screen door had slapped three times behind them.

"She'll take him back, you know," Bobby said, turning to Ike. "He's a Sauls too."

"Most likely," Ike answered. "Come on, let's finish filling this hole. Old Wilkes is doing it all by himself."

The rain quit around midafternoon, but the clouds stayed. The humidity of having the clouds overhead was bad enough even without the sun to steam everything up. Linda and Ronnie stayed inside for four hours, and then Bobby saw Ronnie come out and go to Ike's cottage. He was sure there would be trouble then, but in a few minutes they both appeared, carrying Linda's things back to her old cottage. Ike made three trips and then went back to his place, and they did not hear from him the rest of the day. Wilkes had gone back inside too, and they still did not know what he was going to do, now that the skeleton was finished. Bobby guessed he would go back home and try to pick up his life with his wife because everything else was done, but he couldn't be sure. He didn't know about Ike. He had seemed to give up on Linda too easily, and Bobby didn't like it. Linda was what Ike had stayed around all these months for, but he had not made a sound when Ronnie came back for her. That wasn't like Ike, or maybe it was. Bobby wasn't sure.

Linda came for the baby after the rain had stopped. She offered no information about what had happened, and neither Bobby nor Mother Sauls asked. She simply took Rosebud from Mother and started back across the yard, disappeared into her cottage, and didn't come out for three days.

Bobby sat on the porch and stared at the water, and for the first time in many months, perhaps years, it was enough just to sit and look at the water. There was no need of scenarios, or dreams, or fantasies, and if the world was less interesting that way, it was also more predictable. He looked at the water and tried to make sense of everything that had happened in the last few days. But it was still a mass of confusing emotions, and he gave up on it. Mother Sauls fixed a big pitcher of iced tea and brought it out to the porch, and then she went back inside to her worktable and came back with her manuscript. She sat in the chair next to Bobby with the stack of papers in her lap and poured them each a glass of tea.

"What are you doing with that?" Bobby said, taking the tea from her.

"It's all in here," she said, patting the manuscript. "My whole life, up until just a few years ago, and I realized one thing while I was writing it down."

"What's that?"

"Well, it was supposed to be everything that's ever happened to me, everything I remember, and it is. But dammit, it's also all about you, right from the very beginning. There's no separating the two. It's like Ike said: we're stuck with each other."

"He was saying all that for my benefit," Bobby said. "To have you see me and us in a better light. I told him all about what had happened. He's the only other one I've ever told."

"I know," said Mother Sauls. "But he really didn't have to say anything, you see. It's all right here in what I've written."

"It doesn't mean anything," Bobby said. "Talking about it hasn't changed anything. It's only made it worse. There isn't even that between us anymore." He lit a cigarette and looked at the water. There was a large group of birds working a school of baitfish about a quarter mile out. Bobby could barely make them out as they swooped and dived against the gray sky.

"There's one more thing," said Mother Sauls. "As long as we're telling all. When you went back in the oyster boats that time and there was that thing between us, I turned to someone else for a while."

Bobby closed his eyes, but he could still see the seabirds wheeling and turning against the sky like a giant, slow-moving pinwheel. There was a wrenching and a tearing, but there was no pain.

"I guess it was partly to punish you and partly because I thought I'd lost you," she continued. "But it happened and then it was over and you never knew. It just made the silence harder and more permanent because I couldn't tell you."

Bobby opened his eyes. The birds had moved out on

the water, and he would only see them as small specks of black against the lavender sky, following the fish. The night was coming up from the ground again, like it always did, but it was still day in the sky. There was nothing to say. They were even—and had been all along. He felt something comfortable beginning to occupy the place where the ghost had been for fifty years, the space the night had filled for a time, and finally nothing at all. And he closed his eyes again and saw that the new comfort growing in to fill the space was not the image of the room where it was always morning or the waving brown grass at the mouth of the quiet, black river, but the image of Mother Sauls and the man together and their view of the Gulf down the long yard from the cottage they had used.

"It was Dink," she said.

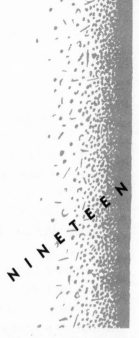

Bobby had a feeling about Psychic Ike early in the morning while he was working on his first pot of coffee. He waited until it was light in the yard and not just on the Gulf, where there were great, towering pink clouds rising on the horizon, and then he went up to Ike's place by the road and knocked on the back screen door. Ike came out right away, and Bobby could tell he was getting ready to leave. He had cleaned out his kitchen and put all the usable canned goods and other items in boxes on the porch, and he was getting together his personal things and the spiritualist stuff in the saddlebags he carried on the bike. Bobby saw that he wasn't taking much with him, and then he remembered that was the way he'd come in too. Ike was used to traveling light.

Ike smiled his big, biker grin and opened the screen door for Bobby. "I'd fix you some coffee, old man," he said. "But I've already packed everything away. Tell Mother everything in the boxes is good stuff. She can use it, or resell it, or whatever. I can't carry it."

"You would have stopped by to say good-bye, wouldn't you?"

"Sure," Ike said. "It's early yet. I still have some things to do. I would have come by."

He turned away, and Bobby followed him into the living room, where he was packing the saddlebags on the floor. All the séance equipment had been removed and packed away, and the room was just a bare, simple cottage again. Ike got on his knees and started stuffing clothes into the bags.

"It's going to be strange," Bobby began. "You've been here a long time. I kind of felt you were family."

Ike looked at him and held held up his right hand, spreading out his five fingers. "Nope," he said. "That can't be, man."

"The finger doesn't matter, Ike. It's just a shitty old deformity, you know."

"It matters," Ike said. "You just don't know yet how much it matters." He got off the floor, crossed to the coffee table, and picked up the last candlestick. Bobby watched him but could think of nothing to say, no way to express the tightness in his throat he knew was for Ike's leaving.

Ike stood up suddenly as if some important thought had just struck him. "You remember that place you took me out in the Gulf?" he said. "That weird freshwater spring? Well, these cottages are just like that, man. Nothing from the outside can stay in here for very long, and you sure can't survive for long out there. You people are tight, man. Real tight. I thought bikers were tight, but you guys got them beat. That's what the finger means, man. If you don't have it, you can't cut it here, no matter how hard you try, so it really does mean everything."

"Did you love her?" Bobby said.

"Hey, who knows, man. It doesn't make any difference now. It's just time to move on, that's all."

"We loved you," Bobby said. "I loved you."

Ike stopped what he was doing and looked at Bobby, and then his eyes turned red and watery and he lowered them. He came to where Bobby was standing and hugged him.

"I love you too, old man. You scrawny little fucker. Come on, let me go say good-bye to Ma."

Bobby touched him on the arm. "One more thing," he said. "Just so I'll know. Can you really see the future?"

"All of it," Ike said.

"Then the prediction's real, isn't it?"

"Of course. But then, you've known that all along, haven't you? You're just too dumb to know where to look."

Ike took up the saddlebags and threw a rolled-up blanket at Bobby for him to carry, and they went out through the kitchen and back porch that looked down the long yard to the Gulf. Psychic Ike tied the things on the bike, straddled the shining, fat machine, and kicked the engine over.

"Climb on," he shouted. "I'll give you the ride of your misguided life."

Bobby got on behind Ike and tried to put his arms around the big man's middle but couldn't reach, so he settled for his wide leather belt and held on as Ike put the bike in gear and accelerated out of the yard and onto the blacktop. There were no cars on the road that early, and Ike steadily pushed the big cycle faster and faster until they were flying over the Ochlockonee Bay Bridge and then he yelled over his shoulder for Bobby to stand up on the pegs, and Bobby did. And suddenly the wind Ike had been breaking hit him full in the face, and he could see the road and the concrete posts of the bridge sucking by. He was afraid and dug his hand farther under Ike's arms to hold on. He looked at the speedometer and saw it register one hundred, and then Ike nudged it up to one-ten and held it there. Bobby passed through the fear and felt a long-suppressed yell coming up from his lungs, and he let it out into the incredible wind over the top of Ike's head all the way into Panacea, where Ike began braking and brought the bike to a standstill on the other side of town, under some pines at the side of the road.

Bobby sat back hard on the seat. "Jesus Fucking Christ," he said, catching his breath.

Ike turned and looked at him. "How 'bout it, huh? That's the way you're supposed to ride, man. Hard out. Remember that."

After the wind of the bike, Bobby could feel the hot muggy air of the real morning on his skin, but the woods off the road were cool and wet, and he could hear them dripping as the sun rose in the trees and the dew fell. "I'll remember," he said. "It was a wonderful ride." He ran his eyes around Ike's mass of hair and beard. "I'm thinking of getting a tattoo," he said.

Ike threw back his head and laughed. "A tattoo? What's it going to say?"

"I don't know." Bobby smiled. "I hadn't thought of that. Maybe I'll just get one that says *Mother*."

Ike laughed again and hugged Bobby. "That's the one, Sauls," he said. "That's the one."

"Where will you go?" Bobby said.

"Somewhere I can stay busy," said Ike. "That's the key, you know. It shuts everything else out. It doesn't really matter what it is, as long as you stay busy."

Bobby looked out into the woods. He could see the sun through the long, wet needles of the pines.

"Well, let's so see Mother," Ike said. "I've got to be getting on the road."

He took them back up the road at a respectable speed, and Bobby could see much of the countryside he'd missed coming down. When they came to the bridge, he stood up on the pegs again, and it was like he was flying under control six feet above the pavement. It was a beautiful morning on the water. To the right he could see up the bay where the river began to narrow, and the fishing camps and marinas there, and to the left, the wide mouth of the bay and then the Gulf and the pale, nearly white horizon, with the color all gone out of the clouds. He filled his lungs with the wonderful mix of smells while they were on the water, and then they came on land again and the smells were altogether different, more woodsy and cool. Bobby took in the air and tasted it on his tongue and remained standing all the way back to the cottages.

Ike turned off the blacktop into the yard and went straight down toward the water and Bobby's cottage. Mother Sauls was out hanging clothes on the line. Bobby could see his extra set of khaki shorts and several of his white tee shirts already hung. The water was blue and still, and he could see birds working the water in three places.

Mother Sauls did not look away from her wash when they rumbled up, but, rather, finished her work as if they weren't there. Ike and Bobby sat on the bike and waited, and then Bobby remembered he wasn't going anywhere and climbed off. Mother Sauls hung the last article of clothing, picked up the wicker clothes basket, and turned to face them.

"So, where to now, Mr. Ike?" she said.

"I'm going to miss you, Mom." Ike smiled. "You're a regular bundle of sentimentality."

"You'd be surprised," she said. "I'll say this—you've helped make this an interesting summer all around."

Ike looked at her a long moment. "You never quit, do you?"

"Can't quit," said Mother Sauls. "The place would float away on some sunny dream."

"Maybe that wouldn't be so bad," Ike said. "Well, come here and give me a hug. I've got to hit the road."

Mother Sauls put down the clothes basket, stepped over to Ike, and hugged him. Ike took up her hand with the extra finger and kissed it, and then he kick started the cycle, waved to them both, and wheeled around to start up the yard. Ronnie had come out of his cottage and was standing in the yard. Ike slowed the Harley and stopped and they shook hands and said something that Bobby couldn't hear, and then Ike was charging up the yard and out onto the road.

Bobby and Mother stood by the clothesline until they could no longer hear the sound of the motorcycle, and then Mother Sauls picked up her basket and started into the house. Ronnie was coming across the yard toward Bobby. He was clean-shaven and rested, and the crazy, distant look Bobby had seen in his eyes in Tallahassee was gone. Ronnie came up to where Bobby was standing and put his hands in his pockets.

"Linda couldn't say good-bye," he said. "It was better that she didn't come out, don't you think?"

"I don't have an opinion on it," Bobby said. "How was jail?"

"It straightened me out," Ronnie said. "I had a few days to think."

Bobby looked at the innocent, dumb face of Ronnie the oysterman and wondered how long it would be before he went crazy again, before he left the hardware job and went back out in the boats, before some other frustration brought out the anger that was always lurking not so far away.

"I'll be around forever," Ronnie said.

Bobby nodded and started walking away toward his own cottage. "Linda told me all about Junior," Ronnie said. "We've been praying for him. We're starting back to church again; maybe you and Mother would like to come along."

Bobby did not stop or turn around or acknowledge Ronnie at all. He just kept going, looking at the Gulf.

Wilkes left in the afternoon. He came to the screen door while Bobby was asleep in his chair on the porch. Mother Sauls let him in. Bobby woke up and saw them standing over him. He thought at first something was wrong, but then he felt the calm in Wilkes, and he sat up and listened.

"I've got the car packed," he said. "I just came to say good-bye and thanks."

"You're welcome," said Mother Sauls. "We wish you luck."

Bobby stood and offered Wilkes his hand. "It was great knowing you," he said. "We don't get too many like you."

"I should hope not." Wilkes laughed. "You know, it was you two that made me decide to go back and try to pull things together."

"Sure," Bobby said. "Ours was a marriage made in heaven."

"Good-bye, Mr. Wilkes," said Mother Sauls. "Take care."

Wilkes shook hands with them both and left. Mother Sauls followed shortly after to get back and mind the store out by the road, and Bobby returned to his chair and settled into the long, hot, empty afternoon. A chameleon crawled up the screen from the palmettos at the base of the porch and then out into the sun on the peeling, horizontal wood frame where the screen was anchored. Bobby watched it turn from bright green to the brown of the wood. It lifted its head and billowed its red, baggy, opaque throat, which glowed with the sunlight through it like a tiny living lamp. And for a moment Bobby felt the same sunlight the lizard was feeling on its bony head and the same dull, white light sheen of its thoughtless brain in which there was almost no activity, and best of all, no memory. And when he opened his eyes the moment had been the whole, transparent afternoon. The chameleon was gone, and Mother Sauls was standing over him with a cold, perspiring beer.

"One of these days I'm going to come out here and find you permanently asleep," she said. "Right here in your little chair. And then the whole thing will be over, and I'm probably going to be very sad."

Bobby took the beer from her and sat up straight in the chair. "I wasn't sleeping," he said. "I was thinking it would be good to go down to the beach and collect some shells. Coquinas, I think."

"I'll pack us some sandwiches and we can eat down at the point," said Mother Sauls. "It will be fun. We haven't done that in a long time."

"We won't make it all the way to the point," Bobby said. "Let's just go together until we get tired, and then we'll turn around."

Bobby drank the beer, and Mother Sauls got a floppy straw hat from the bedroom, and they left the cottage and went down the path to the beach. The sun was low and in their eyes as they walked, but settling in a soft blue and gray haze of streaking, horizontal clouds on the horizon. It lit up the white surf and carved the shells from the sand for them. Where the tide had come up and retreated, there was a line of coquina, like a narrow, broken, winding road. Mother Sauls took off her hat and started placing the tiny shells in it, but Bobby stopped her, took the hat and dumped out the shells.

"Just the blue ones," he said. "Please. I'm going to build a wall. It will give me something to do while I'm waiting."